GW00601579

THE DUKE'S DECISION

Lady Sarah finds Captain Paul Marchand, the Provost Marshal sent to arrest a deserter, an attractive gentleman. But she is, of course, *not* about to throw her cap in his direction ...! She is more concerned with her mama's extraordinary behaviour, and with planning the wedding of her sister Amanda to Richard, the Duke of Denchester. But events do not turn out as planned, and when Paul resigns from the army, everything changes for both of them ...

FENELLA J. MILLER

THE DUKE'S DECISION

Complete and Unabridged

LINFORD
Leicester

First published in Great Britain in 2020

First Linford Edition
published 2022

*A catalogue record for this book is available
from the British Library.*

ISBN 978–1–4448–4822–9

Published by
Ulverscroft Limited
Anstey, Leicestershire

Printed and bound in Great Britain by
TJ Books Ltd., Padstow, Cornwall

This book is printed on acid-free paper

1

June 1810

'Sarah, the carriage is waiting. Why are you loitering in here?' The Dowager Duchess of Denchester said sharply.

'Mama, I don't wish to live at Radley Manor. No Sinclair has ever lived there and I would much prefer to remain here at the Dower House.'

'Poppycock! Your sister cannot hold her wedding breakfast here as everything is constantly covered in the dust from the demolition of the old house. Radley is twice the size of this and far more suitable for a family of our consequence to reside in.'

She could hardly tell her mother the real reason behind her reluctance to leave. Cousin Richard, now the head of the family, had intended to take Amanda to live there when they were married at the end of the month. It didn't seem fair that Mama, their younger sister Beth, and herself plus their various maids and companions should be living with the newly-wedded couple.

When she got married the very last thing she would wish for, was having her family accompany her to her new home. She turned and smiled.

'I'm coming, I apologise for keeping you waiting.'

It was scarcely half an hour's drive and as the weather was clement they were travelling in the brougham. The journey was most enjoyable despite the fact that her mother continued to harangue her for her tardiness.

Something that was said finally registered. 'We could not remain here once Richard and Amanda moved as there would have been no gentleman to oversee matters.'

'Mr O'Riley could have done that.'

'What fustian you speak, my dear. It is high time that we found you a suitable husband. As you are so determined not to return to Town next year and have your Season then I am obligated to find you someone from the locality. With that in mind I have invited several gentlemen to the wedding breakfast who might well be of interest.' Mama intended to have her own way.

★ ★ ★

She hated to argue with her redoubtable parent but summoned up the courage to state her feelings clearly. 'I have no intention of getting married this year or next. And when I do, it will be for Cousin Richard to take charge of the search. I intend to inform him that you have sent invitations, without either Amanda's or his permission, to these families.'

Fortunately, the carriage turned onto the drive and there was no further opportunity for her mother to berate her. Fond as she was of her parent, she was forced to admit that since Mama had been obliged to abandon playing cards for money she was in a permanent bad temper. Amanda was no longer her mama's concern as she was about to be married to the duke, therefore she took her spite out on the one daughter who had no option but to suffer in silence.

Beth, who at seventeen was a year younger than herself, had the mental capacity of a six-year-old child and was usually exempt from any unpleasantness. Miss Westley was now employed as Beth's governess but Nanny remained in the nursery to take care of her sister's every day needs.

The Manor, although not of as recent construction as the Dower House, could not be more than one hundred years of age. Papa had had the building renovated and refurbished and she was assured by Amanda that they would be comfortable there until the new house was built on the site of their ancestral home.

Her sister was waiting in the turning circle to greet them. There was no sign of her future brother-in-law. 'I was beginning to wonder what had happened to you and Mama. Beth and Miss Westley are already exploring their new domain.'

Amanda laughed. 'I've no idea where Richard is, he and Mr O'Riley are somewhere about the estate.'

'I hope you do not intend to keep us waiting on the doorstep, my girl, I am eager to see my apartment. I sincerely hope that it is commensurate with my station in life.'

Sarah exchanged a smile with her sister. 'I'm sure you'll be satisfied with your new accommodation, Mama. Amanda, I assume that I'm not to be sharing with you.'

'We are to share an apartment until I'm actually married to Richard in four weeks' time. Come in and look around your new home.'

The entrance hall was spacious, twice the size of the one at the Dower House and had a remarkable painted ceiling and a wide oak staircase festooned with intricate carvings of beasts, birds and plants.

'I love this. It's quite beautiful. I can see why Richard and you wish to live here for the next two years.'

'I'm glad that you like it, Sarah, as it will be your home too.'

The housekeeper stepped forward and curtsied and then escorted their mama up the stairs. They could hear their parent speaking and none of what she said was complimentary.

'I don't know how you and Richard are going to tolerate her living under your roof when she has been so curmudgeonly since we returned from Town.'

'I have allocated her a delightful drawing room overlooking the garden at the rear of the house where she can sit and entertain her friends. Her apartment is directly above it and in the opposite direction from ours.'

'Do you mean yours and Richard's or the one that you and I are to share until you marry?'

Her sister slipped her arm through hers. 'You must come at once, my love, and see for yourself how I have managed things. Richard and I will have his study for our own use, and there is a music room and the main drawing room for

6

family gatherings. There are also two dining rooms, one for formal occasions and one for breakfast and informal evenings.'

The more Sarah saw of her new abode the better she liked it. 'The rooms are handsome, well-appointed and furnished. I cannot credit that the previous tenant, an old gentleman, had such good taste.'

'Do you not recognise the furniture? Look more closely, my dear.'

'It's from our original home, isn't it? I do recognise a few items but then there were so many rooms it would be hard to recall everything. Wherever it came from, it looks perfectly splendid here.'

She admired again the carved staircase, her bedchamber and shared sitting room, and then they ascended to the nursery floor where Beth, Miss Westley and Nanny were now residing.

Their sister heard them coming and burst out from the schoolroom clapping her hands. 'Isn't this the best house you've ever seen, Sarah?' She pointed to the dolls' house and rocking horse that had accompanied her from the Dower House. 'I have all my favourite things to play with. My room is ever so big. Miss Westley has a bedchamber and a sitting room all to herself. Shall I show you?'

'No, sweetheart, Miss Westley's apartment is private and only for her use. Where is Nanny sleeping?' Amanda put her arm around Beth's waist and guided her back into the chamber that had once been the schoolroom but was now a pretty playroom ideal for their sister's needs.

Sarah was admiring the view which from this height allowed her to look across the park to the woods and farms that accompanied it. She could even see the church tower in the little village nearby.

'Good heavens, come and see, Amanda. There are three red-coated soldiers cantering down the drive.'

'Oh no! Quickly, we must go downstairs. Richard feared that Mr O'Riley would be discovered and that they would send the Provost Marshals for him. I was so hoping that he was now safe, but his five years are not finished until the end of the month.'

Sarah's heart was thudding uncomfortably behind her bodice. 'What do we do? Are we to pretend that we don't know him?'

'We do know Patrick O'Riley, an English gentleman of Irish descent who is employed as the duke's man of affairs. We don't, of course, know anything about the common fellow called Riley who was a sergeant major in the military.'

★ ★ ★

Captain Paul Marchand had not asked for this assignment and wasn't looking forward to confronting the former Major Sinclair, now Duke of Denchester, about his mysteriously vanished sergeant major. 'I think it would be better if we arrived at a more decorous pace, gentlemen,' he told his two companions firmly.

'Yes, sir,' they replied smartly and all

three reined back to a sedate walk.

'Remember to whom we're speaking. His grace has a formidable position in society and we cannot question him aggressively.'

Ensign Robinson grinned. 'From what I hear, captain, one wouldn't want to have upset him before his elevation. He had a fearsome reputation as Major Sinclair.'

The other member of his small party remained silent as was only appropriate for an enlisted man.

'I don't understand why Horse Guards is so determined to reclaim Riley. Good God — he has less than a month to go on his five years. There has to be more to this than we know.'

'Did you ever meet either of them, sir?'

'I never had the pleasure. However, Riley will not be hard to identify as he has red hair and is as tall as me.'

They were approaching the handsome building but there was no sign that they had been seen. The front door remained firmly closed against them. Either the family were out or intended to make things as difficult as possible. He smiled wryly. If he was in Sinclair's shoes, he would be equally uncooperative.

The information he had about Riley was that he had been with his grace for several years and they were good friends now. Therefore, it would hardly be surprising if the duke refused to cooperate. One thing that was not in doubt, as far as was concerned, was that Riley had most likely remained with Sinclair.

This was not the career Paul had intended or hoped for. The price of a captaincy in a regiment had been beyond his means and when this was offered, he had transferred from the light infantry to the Provost Marshals with alacrity. He was now sincerely regretting his decision.

Rounding up mutinous soldiers, searching for deserters, arresting enlisted men who ran rampant in a captured city would have been a worthwhile and respectable way to spend his time. Being sent here to arrest someone like Riley, who had served his country faithfully for

11

years, did not sit well with him.

It had been made abundantly clear to him that if he failed in his first assignment he would be immediately demoted, if not cashiered. Why the hell was General Boyden so insistent that Riley return to his regiment? It didn't make sense. By the time Riley was returned to Horse Guards he would have completed his five years and be a free man.

Tarnation take it! Riley could still be hung as a deserter but would be offered the alternative of signing on for a further five years and would have no option but to take this or die. General Boyden must think very highly of this man to go to such lengths to have him re-enlist. The man had been a professional soldier most of his adult life and Paul was certain, even if he was forced back into the military, he would serve with the same dedication he had previously.

Walking the horses the last half a mile had been sensible as they were now cool and could be fed and watered immediately. He dismounted smoothly and tossed his reins to the third member of their party, Private Brown. This man was a surly individual and he didn't trust him.

'Take the horses around to the stables and see to them. You can make enquiries there about Riley, but do it politely. Is that understood?'

The man nodded but didn't respond. There was going to be trouble with him if Paul couldn't deal with his insolence. Their overnight baggage had been left with the packhorse, and the spare mount for the prisoner, at a decent hostelry in a village a mile from here.

'Knock on the door, Ensign Robinson. I'll remain here. I've no wish to appear too eager to apprehend this so-called deserter.'

Robinson hammered on the brass dolphin-shaped knocker so enthusiastically that it startled the doves from the trees that bordered the drive. There was no danger that the occupants wouldn't know someone wished to be admitted.

He had the distinct feeling he was

being observed but had no intention of gawping at the windows to see who it might be. Instead he straightened to a military position, put his shako under his arm, and remained eyes firmly front.

There was a considerable delay before the door opened and a frosty-faced gentleman in the garb of a butler enquired their business.

'Captain Marchand wishes to speak to his grace at the earliest opportunity.'

'His grace is not here. He has not deigned to inform me as to his whereabouts or when he intends to return.'

Then we wish to speak to Mr Riley.'

'There is no one of that name residing here.' The wretched man nodded and closed the door firmly in Robinson's face.

The young man raised his fist prepared to demand entry but Paul called him back. 'No, there's no need to pursue this. If the duke's away from home then you can be certain that Riley is with him. We shall remain here until he returns.'

Sarah moved away from the window certain she hadn't been seen. 'The two officers are wandering off towards the stables where the other one took their horses. I don't think they're leaving.'

'Neither do I. I just hope that Richard and O'Riley have the sense to remain away from here until tomorrow. The soldiers cannot stay after dark and I've no intention whatsoever of inviting them to come in.'

The strident tones of their mother interrupted the conversation. 'To whom are you referring, Amanda?'

'The Provost Marshals have come to arrest Mr O'Riley. They are lurking about in the grounds in the hope that Richard will bring him back before nightfall.'

'And if he doesn't? Pray, what do you intend to do about the officers?'

'I assume they will return from whence they came and try again tomorrow.'

'I think you should invite them in. At least that way, my dear, Richard and Mr

O'Riley will not be caught unawares. I'm sure that you and Sarah can keep them distracted.'

Sarah had been about to suggest the same thing. She couldn't believe the handsome officer who had remained ramrod straight, looking neither right nor left, was anything but a pleasant gentleman. There was something about his bearing, his wide shoulders, his long lower limbs, and especially his open features and dark hair, that engendered a feeling of trust within her bosom.

'I think you might be right, Mama. They will be royally entertained and no doubt when Richard and O'Riley do return they will be warned . . . '

'What is it, Amanda? What has distressed you about this suggestion?'

'We can hardly invite the common soldier into the house, Sarah, so he will remain out there and raise the alarm.'

'Fiddlesticks!' Mama said firmly. 'I do not know much about enlisted men but one thing I am quite certain of is that if they are offered hard liquor, they will imbibe far more than is good for them.'

'Thank you, I should have thought of that myself. The man must be invited into the servants' quarters downstairs and plied with brandy.'

Sarah wasn't sure this was going to work. 'Surely, someone as lowly as he would never be offered brandy? He would immediately suspect something was amiss.'

Her mother snorted inelegantly. 'My dear girl, I was hardly going to suggest that the housekeeper handed him a decanter of Richard's best brandy. The man will be invited in to eat with the stable hands and given the opportunity to steal a decanter.'

It was now her sister's turn to interrupt. 'That will not work, Mama. And even if it would, I'm not going to put the private soldier in such an invidious position. Good heavens, he could be transported or worse for such a crime.'

Their mother's lips pursed, she tossed her head and marched off without another word obviously displeased by the fact that both of them had disagreed with her.

Sarah held her breath until they were once more alone and able to talk freely. 'Getting him drunk seems a good option, but I cannot see how it might be done without alerting him or getting him put on a charge for drunkenness.'

'Then we must come up with another scheme before we invite the officers into the house to dine with us. I think I might ask for two chambers to be prepared as having them under our roof would be safer than allowing them to wander about the countryside. There is a distinct possibility they might come face-to-face with Mr O'Riley.'

'You cannot do that, sister, as they do not have their overnight luggage with them.'

Amanda laughed. 'How very observant of you, my love. Is there anything else you wish to impart about the appearance or behaviour of the officer?'

Sarah's cheeks were hot. 'I am discovered. He is a prodigiously attractive and I would dearly like to meet him despite the reason he's here.'

'I have come up with something that I think might work. What if we invite them in and then let slip that Richard and Mr O'Riley have gone to Ipswich on business? Do you not think the senior man would then send one of his men to investigate?'

'Indeed, I think that would work perfectly. Do you actually know where your betrothed has gone?'

'I have no notion, but I think his unexpected and rapid departure has something to do with the arrival of these men. It's highly unlikely either of them will return until these unwanted visitors have given up and gone to look elsewhere.'

'Something has occurred to me. We're assuming that they already know for certain that Sergeant Major Riley and Mr O'Riley are the same person. Surely, this would be the first place they would look? After all the two of them served together for years.'

'How silly of me. Since I agreed to

marry Richard I'm finding it hard to concentrate on anything but my forthcoming nuptials. We're just confirming his suspicions if we refuse to let him enter — if we have nothing to hide then we would have welcomed them in.'

2

'Your grace, we can't hide out here until the end of the month. You must go back and say that I've gone away on business for you.' Patrick O'Riley was lounging on the grass next to Richard whilst the horses grazed happily on the long grass in the meadow.

'With hindsight I think it a bad move to not have been there when the marshals arrived. It's tantamount to admitting that they're correct in assuming you've remained with me.' He spat out the stalk of grass he had been chewing reflectively. 'Not only that, we've put the ladies in an invidious position. I think we must return as if there's nothing amiss and brazen it out.'

'It would have helped if we knew if we'd ever met any of the arresting party, sir. Being called by a different name and having brown hair instead of red will not be enough to deceive anyone who has made my acquaintance.'

'True.' Richard rose smoothly to his feet and whistled for his horse to return. He was now riding his beloved stallion which had been fetched for him from Corunna and Patrick had his gelding, Rufus. 'Stay here. I'll say you're about your legitimate business but should be back this evening if they have the temerity to enquire. I'll send a groom for you if it's safe for you to return. In fact, I'll send someone anyway to let you know what's going on.'

As he cantered down the leafy lanes he rehearsed in his head what he would say to these gentlemen. Even if he had never met them in person, they would know of his reputation. This should stand him in good stead.

Since he had resigned his colours on discovering that not only had he inherited a dukedom, but also the responsibility for three young ladies and their mother, his world had been turned upside down. He had been reluctant to take up his responsibilities and determined to return to his duties as Major Sinclair. However, fate had determined otherwise.

His lips curved when he recalled how surprised he had been to discover he was the image of the distant relative who had been the previous Duke of Denchester. The fact that he was also the masculine equivalent of Lady Amanda Sinclair, soon to be his beloved wife, had also been a surprise.

Within a short space of time he was neck over crop in love with the girl, but she had taken a deal of persuading to agree to marry him. It was purgatory remaining out of her bed when they were residing under the same roof. He was counting the hours until he had the right to make love to her.

They'd left by the tradesmen's track but he returned down the drive. A groom appeared from under the stable archway to take his stallion.

'I was to tell you, your grace, that there's two officers inside visiting and a common soldier what has gone to look for a person called Sergeant Major Riley what we've never heard of.'

'Thank you, Jethro, your communication is duly noted.'

He strolled to the front door puzzled as to why Amanda had invited the enemy inside. No doubt he would discover this for himself as soon as he set foot indoors. The front door swung open and a liveried footman bowed him in. He tossed the servant his gloves and whip. He never bothered with a hat nowadays.

The drawing room was to the right of the spacious hall and immediately he could hear Amanda and Sarah laughing gaily in response to something one of the officers had said. His smile vanished. He stepped into the chamber, his eyes hard and his expression arctic.

Two redcoats shot to their feet as if stabbed in the derrière by a bayonet and both saluted as if he was still in uniform. They were strangers to him — which was a considerable relief in the circumstances.

Sarah looked nervous but Amanda raised an eyebrow and shook her head.

He relaxed and smiled. 'Good afternoon, gentlemen. You have the advantage of me.'

The taller of the two, a captain, half-bowed. 'Captain Paul Marchand, at your service, your grace. Please allow me to introduce Ensign Robinson.'

He nodded. 'I thought my connection with Horse Guards to be over. If you have been sent to try and persuade me to rejoin my regiment . . .'

'No, your grace, we are in search of your former sergeant major who is designated as a deserter. We were hoping you could enlighten us as to his whereabouts.'

'I thought him returned to duty. I've had no contact with anyone of that name. I am afraid that you have had a wasted journey.' He turned to Amanda. 'I hope you have invited these gentlemen to dine with us, my dear. It's been too long since I heard anything of my former comrades and am eager to catch up on the gossip.'

'Gossip, Richard? I thought that was a female's prerogative. Yes, Captain

Marchand and Ensign Robinson have kindly agreed to stay and dine. If you'll excuse us, gentlemen, I must inform her grace that there will be two extra for dinner today.'

She took Sarah out with her and for some reason the girl seemed reluctant to leave. Her cheeks were pink and he had a nasty suspicion she was, like many other young ladies before her, interested in a handsome young officer.

* * *

Paul was wary of this impressive gentleman. There was nothing soft or effete about this aristocrat — he was military to his backbone.

'Your grace, we are intruding. I am certain that you do not really wish to dine with us and we will make ourselves scarce.'

A glimmer of amusement flickered across the duke's face. 'Not at all, Captain, since I left Corunna I've had little opportunity to discuss my former life.

In fact, if I'm honest, I'm sadly deprived of sensible masculine conversation.' His grace gestured towards the seats the girls had recently vacated. 'Be seated, we have an hour before I need to change for dinner.'

This was not a request but an order and he and his companion hastily resumed their places. He was surprised that their host had not first retreated to his apartment and repaired his appearance. It was impossible to ignore the smell of sweat and horse that drifted towards them.

His expression must have betrayed his thoughts as the duke laughed out loud.

'Is it so bad? I beg your pardon. I should not have come in the drawing room in my dirt.' He remained where he was which surprised Paul. 'It hardly seems worth the bother of going to my rooms now when I shall have to do so shortly to improve my appearance before we dine. The ladies put on something pretty, but not evening gowns, and I do as much as I must to be acceptable.'

'We can do nothing about our appearance, your grace, which is another reason

27

I think it best if we depart.'

'Stay here tonight. Send your ensign to collect your bags. You can set off first thing rested and replete.' The duke looked pointedly at Robinson. 'Where were you intending to stay?'

'The Rising Sun, in the village, no more than a mile from here.'

'Excellent. Ensign Robinson, you can be back in ample time for you both to be able to smarten your appearance and not let down your regiment.'

Again, this was more a command than a suggestion. Paul nodded to Robinson who scrambled to his feet, bowed and hurried out. He relaxed as he realised that they would hardly have been invited to stay if the duke was harbouring a fugitive.

'When do you expect your new abode to be completed? I could see nothing through the dust when I called there first and got your direction.'

'Two years — which is why I have moved the family to Radley Manor. Tell me, Marchand, why has an intelligent young officer chosen to serve as a provost marshal?'

'I had not the wherewithal to purchase a captaincy anywhere else, your grace. I am a career soldier and if I am ever to have a wife and family of my own, I need to climb the ladder and become a major at the least.'

'Would you prefer to be performing your duties on the Peninsular?'

'Indeed I would, sir.' He hesitated not sure if he should reveal more about his thoughts. He came to a decision. He trusted this man would explain what he thought was the reason for him being sent to arrest the errant Sergeant Major Riley.

'General Boyden is behind my search. I believe that he's going to threaten to hang your former sergeant major unless he agrees to sign up for a further term of service. The only positive aspect of this must be that the general thinks very highly of him.'

'I agree with your assessment of the situation. Mr Riley has only to remain out of your hands for a further four weeks and then he will be a free man.'

'Technically perhaps, your grace, but the army will view it differently. I know of instances when deserters have been arrested a year or more after their disappearance and when they are no longer officially members of the army.'

The duke's eyes narrowed. 'That is always a possibility, of course. However, he has friends in high places and I think the general is going to be disappointed.' His lips curved but his eyes remained unfriendly. 'Now, you must tell me what it was you were regaling to my future wife and my ward when I came in a while ago. I could hear them laughing immoderately.'

Paul swallowed and cleared his throat. 'Lady Amanda had just been telling us about an amusing incident that involved her falling asleep in the woods. I then told them about the occasion when I fell asleep on duty.'

'I imagine that the outcome of that was not as amusing,' the duke said dryly.

'I had a bucket of water tipped over my head and was told I was lucky it hadn't been something more malodorous.'

'You are lucky you weren't put on a charge.' The duke's smile was now genuine. 'I doubt that you repeated the offence.'

'No, sir, I certainly didn't. My regiment was about to depart for Portugal and I was eagerly anticipating being able to lead men into battle for the first time. Then this opportunity was offered and I had no recourse but to accept.'

'Have you been told what would be the outcome if you fail in your mission?'

'I will be cashiered at the worst and demoted at the best. Believe me, your grace, I don't agree with my orders but have no option but to follow them.'

'Where have you sent your private soldier? Is he lurking around the stables in the hope of making an arrest?'

'Lady Amanda said that she thought that our man had been sent to Ipswich on business.' Hastily he corrected himself. 'Your man of business, coincidentally called Mr O'Riley, is a person of interest to us. As soon as we have spoken to him, and confirmed that he is not the man we're looking for, then we will leave and continue our search elsewhere.'

'My man will be back tomorrow or the next day. Lady Amanda was incorrect as he has gone to Norwich, not Ipswich. I'm happy to have you and your ensign stay here and your private soldier can find a billet with my outside men.' He stood and Paul had no option but to do the same. 'I have business to attend to before dinner. A servant will show you to your room.'

'Thank you, your grace, I appreciate your hospitality. Do I have your permission to take a walk in your gardens?'

The duke looked at him as if he was speaking in tongues. 'Permission? Good God, man, I'm not your superior. You're my guest and can do as you please.'

Paul could hear him laughing as he wandered off and his cheeks flushed. His grace might no longer be a major in the army but he was definitely his superior in every way. Not only was he a duke and immensely wealthy but also several years older than him and quite probably more intelligent too.

The French doors at the far end of the drawing room were open and he scuttled out. He found himself on a spacious terrace which was edged by a stone balustrade and had a matching stone staircase down into the rose garden. If he wasn't mistaken there was a maze to the left of the ornamental lake and he decided to walk there until he'd recovered his aplomb.

★　★　★

Sarah escaped from her sister, who was waylaid by the housekeeper about some boring domestic detail, and ran upstairs. It was too soon to change for dinner so she would put on her bonnet and boots and take a turn in the garden. The weather was perfect for a stroll.

'Lady Sarah, you should take your parasol, you must stay out of the sun,' her abigail said.

'Very well, if you insist. We have guests tonight so please find me something elegant to wear. I'll be back in good time.'

She left through the door in the music room that opened onto the terrace and hesitated for a moment not sure in which direction to go. A flash of red caught her eye and she realised the handsome officer was in the maze.

Without a second thought she picked up her skirts and ran across the grass to join him. Although he was tall enough to peer over the top of the neatly clipped yew hedges that formed the walls of the maze, he had neglected to take in the wooden flag that could be waved if one became disorientated.

She had once spent an hour trying to find her way out before being rescued by one of the gardeners. The captain would be most embarrassed if he was obliged to shout for assistance.

'Captain Marchand, are you lost in there? Do you wish me to fetch someone who is familiar with the layout?'

She was too short to see where he was but she could hear him moving about. Then the top of his head appeared over the greenery. 'I am about to enter the centre of this structure. I was determined to find it before I come out. I am not lost and do not require assistance although I should be delighted to stroll around in here with you if you are, of course, able to find me.'

'Remain where you are, sir, and I will be with you directly. I cannot resist a challenge.'

'Follow my voice, my lady, that will make it simpler for you.'

He was speaking to her as if she was a child and not a woman grown. 'Captain Marchand, I have been in and out of here several times and have no need to be guided by someone with no knowledge of this maze.'

Her tart retort should have silenced him but instead he laughed which incensed her more. She was determined to give him a severe set down for his patronising words and for laughing at her. In her hurry her skirts became entangled in the hedge and she was travelling so fast that when she was halted so abruptly, she lost her balance. With a despairing cry she tumbled backwards.

The next thing she knew she was sitting on the path, her gown quite ruined and her ankle severely injured. She bit her lip trying not to cry out with the pain. She barely had time to draw another breath before he appeared beside her.

'Remain still, my lady, let me untangle you and examine your ankle before you attempt to stand.'

Without a by your leave he reached around her and released her torn skirts. Then he gently straightened her leg and inspected the injury. Having a gentleman's hands encircle her limb gave her palpitations.

He was so close she could reach out and touch the top of his shining dark hair. The roughness of his regimental coat was brushing her arm. She closed her eyes unable to say anything coherent.

'I don't think it's broken, my dear, just severely sprained. Put your arm around my neck. I'll carry you back.'

'I don't think you should do that. Richard will be most displeased with both of us.'

He sat back on his heels and studied her. 'I think he would be even more displeased if I left you here. Now, cut rope, do as you're told.'

'You have no right to issue orders as if I was one of your enlisted men. I get quite enough of that from my cousin, thank you very much. Go away, I shall be perfectly happy sitting here until someone more suitable comes to my aid.' She had spoken without thought and expected him to ignore her instructions.

To her horror he straightened, nodded politely, and vanished leaving her stranded. He was a most objectionable young man and should have realised she had spoken in anger and didn't mean him to leave her alone.

Her ankle throbbed, the scratches on her arms were bleeding and sore and she sincerely regretted her outburst. She sniffed and rubbed her eyes with her hand.

'Did you really think I would leave you here? Are you ready to comply?'

Obediently she put her hand around his neck, he put one arm about her waist and the other under her knees and she was lifted as if she weighed nothing at all. Somehow he managed to extricate them both from the maze with no difficulty, and without causing her further pain. He had even had the forethought to tuck her torn skirt around her legs so she was revealing nothing that she shouldn't.

They were halfway to the house when Richard appeared. He was at their side in moments. 'God's teeth! You've only been here an hour or two, Marchand, and you're already causing mayhem.' He reached out to take her but to her astonishment the captain shook his head.

'Thank you, your grace, but I can manage perfectly well. Lady Sarah tripped and sprained her ankle in the maze.'

Her cousin's lips thinned. He wasn't

used to being gainsaid. He remained in front of them. Her lethargy vanished as she looked at each of them in turn.

'I will not be handed about like a parcel. Remove yourself, cousin, and allow the captain to continue.'

If before Richard had been annoyed, now he was astonished. This was the first time she'd had the temerity to argue with him although her sister did so all the time. Then he smiled.

'I beg your pardon, Sarah. Captain take her to her apartment and her maids can attend her there.'

3

Richard stepped aside reluctantly. Something about this officer made alarm bells ring. On first acquaintance he had appeared well-mannered, suitably respectful, but that was a façade. The pleasant, smiling countenance had momentarily fooled him. He now bitterly regretted his casual invitation for them to stay as long as they liked.

He had sent a groom to tell Patrick to remain at the Dower House until told otherwise. What the devil had Sarah been doing in the maze with Marchand?

On entering the house, he snapped his fingers and gave his instructions. He stood in the hall and watched the young officer move easily up the stairs with the girl in his arms. They both seemed inordinately pleased about the situation.

He could hardly toss the man out but having him under the same roof as his ward for the next few days was a recipe for disaster. Sarah was halfway to being enamoured of the officer already — he had no notion what Marchand's feelings might be on the subject. Was it possible that he had already seen a golden opportunity to marry money and be able to buy himself a better position in the army?

The tall-case clock against the far wall struck the hour. Dammit to hell! If he was to change his raiment and be down in time for dinner then he had better get on with it. He refused to put on evening clothes but had agreed to spruce himself up a bit and not appear in the items he had been wearing all day.

Instead of going to his apartment he walked down the passageway and knocked on the bedchamber door of his future wife. He needed to speak to her immediately.

The door opened and he stepped past the maid not waiting for permission to enter. 'Sweetheart, I'm sorry to disturb you.'

She was in her shift and every curve and roundness was evident beneath the thin material. Most young women would have been horrified by his intrusion but she laughed.

'Please come in, my love,' she said with a sweet smile.

As he was already inside the chamber, he laughed out loud. 'Baggage. Your sister has twisted her ankle — I don't think it's too serious — but I'm concerned about her involvement with that captain.'

She gestured to her maid to leave and snatched up her bedrobe and pulled it on before answering. 'What happened to alarm you?'

He explained and if he'd hoped she would dispel his concerns he would have been disappointed.

'Oh dear! Where young ladies are concerned an attractive officer in a red coat is to be avoided at all costs. Sarah's not like me, she's a romantic and could well imagine herself in love with him having spent only an hour in his company. I thought him an intelligent and well-spoken gentleman. I wish now I'd not invited him to stay.'

'As do I, sweetheart. The fact that he rescued her will just add flames to the fire. That's not the only problem. I underestimated him and now believe he hasn't been fobbed off so easily. I fear that Patrick will be apprehended and forced to re-enlist.'

'It was inevitable that they came to look here first. We would have been better sending him to one of the estates in the north.'

'As always, my darling, you have come up with the perfect solution. I'll send him to Scotland. I noticed I have a property in Edinburgh and I doubt they would ever find him there.'

'From what you've told me, Richard, he could still be arrested at any time even after his time is done. How are you going to put this right?'

'I shall write to London, to Horse Guards, and hope I can persuade them to let the matter drop. If I offer to pay a substantial sum to recompense them for his loss then I'm sure I'll be able to get him released without charge.' He frowned. 'Maybe it would be better to deliver the letters in person.'

'Then as soon as we can be rid of these unwanted guests you must go immediately. I can deal with any problems that might arise in your absence. Which reminds me, my mother's becoming unbearable. Perhaps you should send her away as you once threatened to do. Mr O'Riley can act as her escort.'

'Are you saying that you don't wish her to attend our wedding?'

'Frankly, if her behaviour doesn't improve then I would prefer her not to be there. I cannot credit that being denied the opportunity to gamble has caused this change in her.'

'Remember I told you about the man who actually punched his commanding officer when he was denied the right to gamble. I think we must live with the bad temper and hope that in time she will adjust to the new reality.'

She looked at him, her eyes wide. 'You're being remarkably sanguine, my love, and I thank you for it. I think she's the least of our problems now. I'll go at once to speak to Sarah and see how she does. Fortunately, as she has sprained her ankle, she must remain upstairs tonight. In the circumstances I consider this a good thing.'

He turned to leave then reconsidered. In two strides he was across and swept her into his arms. 'Waiting for our wedding night is becoming more difficult every day.' He kissed her and she responded. Somehow he managed to untangle himself before things got out of hand. 'I love you, darling girl, but my willpower is evaporating like snow on a summer's day.'

'How poetic, Richard, but your comparison makes no sense at all. Go away and let me get dressed.'

He was still chuckling when he met up with the young captain. His smile faded.

'Your grace, Lady Sarah wishes to speak to you.' He nodded and walked past as if he owned the place, not waiting for a response.

Richard walked into the sitting room

that Sarah shared with her sister and found her resting on the *chaise longue* with her injured ankle elevated and wrapped in what looked like a wet cloth.

'You wish to speak to me, sweetheart? How can I be of assistance?'

'It wasn't Captain Marchand's fault that I had this accident. It was I that rushed into the maze after him not the other way around.'

He perched on the end of the daybed and folded his arms. 'If that remark is supposed to reassure me, young lady, then you're short of the mark. It has done the reverse.'

She didn't meet his eye and fiddled with her sash. 'I cannot imagine why I went after him. I didn't think I was the sort of girl to be overwhelmed by an attractive man in scarlet regimentals. Obviously, I was wrong.' She looked up, her eyes glittered and he felt a brute. 'You have no need to worry about my behaving immodestly again as I have every intention of remaining in my room until both officers have gone. I apologise

46

for my behaviour.'

'You'll do no such thing, little one. Stay here tonight if you wish, but I'm quite prepared to carry you downstairs. Tomorrow you should be able to put weight on that injury but I'm still prepared to act as your transport if necessary.'

'I might have given the wrong idea to Captain Marchand and I'm too embarrassed to see him again.'

'I can assure you he will treat you with the utmost respect. You will not be alone with him again so there's no danger of you doing anything inappropriate.'

★ ★ ★

Sarah managed a feeble smile. 'Thank you, Richard, for being so understanding. You have every right to be angry with me.'

'I couldn't be angry with you for more than a moment. Now, do you wish to go down to dine or are you having a tray upstairs?'

'I think I prefer to stay here tonight but if I cannot walk unaided then I would be grateful to be assisted in the morning.'

He ruffled her hair as he walked out and she thought, not for the first time, how lucky her sister was to be marrying him. She rather thought her interest in the captain had been because Richard had once been a major in the army himself.

The connecting door to her sister's bedchamber opened and Amanda walked in looking particularly beautiful in a dark green gown with light green embroidery around the hem, neck and sleeves.

'I love that ensemble, Amanda, have you dressed to impress our visitors?'

'Of course I have. I am the future Duchess of Denchester and cannot be seen abroad anything but perfect. Are you quite sure you don't wish to come down? I heard Richard offer to carry you and I'm quite happy to help you change as there's still time.'

'No, I've made a complete nincompoop of myself this afternoon and intend to remain here until the military gentle-men have left.'

'Fiddlesticks to that! They could be here for several days and I'm not having you hiding in your bedchamber for that long. You will come down tomorrow whether you wish to or not.'

Sarah was quite relieved that her sister had insisted. 'Then I will agree. I'm hoping I shall be able to walk with just your arm to lean on. I really didn't enjoy being carried about the place.'

'Is that so? I think I would have found the experience pleasurable. I must ask Richard to carry me somewhere so that I can make up my mind.'

'You must go down, Amanda, it would not do to be tardy. Especially as our mama is in such high dudgeon at the moment.'

'I shan't remain to entertain them with a performance on the piano however much I might be asked. I shall be back as soon as dinner is over.' With a cheerful wave she drifted out of the room and Sarah could hear her laughing and talking to someone in the passageway.

Her cheeks coloured as she realised it was the captain. Why was he in their part of the house when his rooms were on the far side? Surely he hadn't intended to visit her? That would be most irregular. Despite her determination to cordially dislike him her heart skipped a beat or two. She sighed and settled back to think about what had occurred that afternoon.

It wasn't as if she hadn't been introduced and danced with several eligible and handsome young gentlemen whilst in London, but this was her first — if one didn't count Mr O'Riley and Richard — encounter with an actual officer in uniform.

The evening seemed interminable and her usual healthy appetite deserted her and she was only able to pick at the delectable morsels sent up to her on a tray. Miss Westley, who had once been governess to herself and Amanda, came in to see her.

'Lady Sarah, you have hardly touched your tray. Does your ankle pain you so much you cannot eat?'

'I find that I'm not hungry tonight. We rarely have guests to dine I would so liked to have been there.'

'That was your choice, my dear, as I know that either his grace or the captain would have been only too pleased to carry you downstairs.'

'Did you see them? I'm surprised you weren't asked to join the party.'

'Good heavens, a governess does not dine with the family unless it is to make up numbers. Now, let me remove that tray and I shall read to you. I have brought down the latest novel that arrived only yesterday from Hatchards in London. I've read the first chapter and am already engrossed.'

'I hope you don't intend to start the second and leave me to guess what happened previously.'

'Don't worry, I've no intention of doing that.'

Despite the fact that the story was exciting, the hero dark and disreputable, the heroine in dire need of rescuing, Sarah could not enjoy the book. Her ankle ached deplorably and she fidgeted and sighed until Miss Westley put the book down.

'I shall go at once to the kitchen and find you a soothing tisane as you are obviously in a lot of discomfort. I wonder if we should send for the physician.'

'It's not broken, just sprained and painful. What I'd really like is some lemonade if there's any to be found. I know there are lemons on the trees in the orangery and I'm sure that Cook could easily make me some if you would be kind enough to take her the fruit.'

'I'll leave the book here, Lady Sarah, you might find it more appealing if you read it to yourself.'

The governess, who was also a dear friend, hurried off leaving her alone. She flexed her foot and immediately regretted it. She leaned across and rang the little brass bell that had been put beside her by her maid.

'How can I help, my lady?'

'I need to use the commode. If I hop and you hold on to me, I think I can manage to reach it without falling again.'

By the time she was done she was biting her lip wishing she was safely in her bed. Her abigail tutted and fussed but eventually was able to assist her into the bedchamber.

'There now, my lady, you sit on your bed and I'll help you disrobe. Your ankle is ever so swollen and blue — I do hope you haven't broken it.'

'So do I, but I'm beginning to fear that I might have. I'm hoping that when her grace or Lady Amanda come to see me later that they will fetch me some laudanum.'

'Laudanum, sweetheart? Is your ankle so painful that you need to take that?' Richard came in carrying the tray of lemonade. It was typical of him to play the role of servant. He stood on no ceremony and did as he pleased which was one reason she was so fond of him.

'I don't like to make a fuss, but the pain is far worse than it was and I cannot move it at all.'

He frowned and put the tray down. 'I

should have looked at it myself not taken your word that the damage wasn't serious.'

Her maid hastily folded back the sheet from the bottom making sure that no more than her ankle was visible.

'Devil take it! I fear that could be more than a sprain. Small wonder you're in agony — it needs to be splinted just in case.' He rubbed the tears from her cheeks with his thumb. 'Be brave, sweetheart, I've set bones for my men many times and can do it as efficiently as a sawbones. Sit tight and I'll fetch what I need.'

She managed to smile. 'I can do nothing else, Richard. May I have some laudanum or do you disapprove of its use?'

'My men would drink a flask of cognac to deaden the pain. I think you would be better with a small amount of laudanum.' He left the sheet folded back, smiled reassuringly, and bounded out of the room.

Despite her pain her lips curved as

she heard him yelling through the house. Five minutes later there were running footsteps outside and her sister burst in.

'You should have told me how much pain you are in, my love. Richard has gone to find the items he needs and I have your pain relief.' Amanda carefully tipped a few drops into a glass of lemonade and handed it to her. 'Our mother is playing cards with the officers.'

'Then I don't expect her to visit me tonight. I'm so sorry to have caused this upset. It took you weeks to recover from your broken leg and I've no wish to spoil your nuptials.'

'Nothing will do that, Sarah, I can assure you. I'm certain that I saw a bath chair in the attic and I'll have it brought down for you. Even if you cannot walk you'll not miss my marriage.' She squeezed her hand. 'Anyway, it might not be broken. Richard is being cautious.'

He came in and set about the unpleasant task of splinting her ankle. Amanda held her hand and she did her best not to whimper but the pain was so severe her head swam and everything went black. When she came around he was done. From somewhere they had found a basket cradle upon which to place the covers so they didn't touch her injury.

'You will have to stay off that until a doctor has seen it. I'm sorry to have hurt you, little one, but you will be more comfortable now.'

* * *

Paul enjoyed a hand of cards as much as the next gentleman but after an hour he was beginning to find the intensity of the dowager alarming. Her eyes were gleaming and every trick she took, even though they were playing for pennies, appeared to increase her determination to win.

'Now, gentlemen, shall we make this more interesting? The duke and my daughter have now gone so we can please ourselves.' She then suggested they played for more than he could afford and certainly way above the means of Robinson.

'Unfortunately, your grace, we have not the wherewithal to increase the stakes.'

'I am prepared to accept a written note for any debts you might have accrued over the evening.'

He had no wish to cause offence but he wasn't going to be bullied into doing something he didn't want to. He put down his cards and Robinson did the same.

'I thank you for a pleasant evening, your grace, but my ensign and I have had a long day and are going to retire.'

He was on his feet, bowed, and was heading for the door before she had time to protest. Their exit was so precipitous he almost collided with his host.

'I was coming to find you.' He glanced over his shoulder and his expression changed from pleasant to alarming. 'Lady Sarah has possibly broken her ankle so I have stabilised it with a splint. Excuse me, gentlemen, I need to speak to my future mother-in-law.'

The duke stepped into the drawing room and closed both doors firmly behind him. 'We are *de trop*, shall we take a stroll in the garden before we go up?'

'Yes, sir, I need to clear my head.'

They didn't speak again until they were safely outside and walking across the damp grass. 'Thank you for extricating us from that situation, sir, we could have lost a fortune tonight if you hadn't done so.'

'Her grace is, I believe, a hardened gambler. However, I'm certain his grace would have stepped in before we were in above our heads. He's obviously aware of the problem.'

'I've not met a duke before but I'm certain that he doesn't behave like one.'

Paul smiled in the darkness. 'He is an officer first and an aristocrat second. I like the man but I'm convinced that he's harbouring our quarry. Mr O'Riley, his man of affairs, sounds remarkably like Riley in appearance apart from his hair being brown and not red.'

'How can we prove that as we haven't met him before?'

'Unfortunately, I must write to Horse

Guards and have them send someone here who knew him in his former persona.' He swore under his breath. 'Not that that will do any good as I'm certain he won't return here until after we've departed.'

'So what are we going to do?'

Paul was about to tell his young subordinate but decided against it. There was no need for both of them to be cashiered.

4

Richard strode across the drawing room and towered over the Dowager Duchess. 'Madam, I thought I made it abundantly clear that you will not play cards for money.'

She remained silent for a moment fiddling with the cards and the pile of pennies in front of her. He was hopeful that his stern reprimand would be enough. Then she surged to her feet sending the card table crashing to the floor.

'How dare you speak to me like that? I will not tolerate such insolence from you or anyone else. How I wish to spend my time and my money is none of your concern.'

He ignored her outburst and calmly righted the table — he left the cards and coins for the servants to collect. 'I think that you forget to whom you speak. I am the head of the family and my word is law if you wish to remain under my

60

roof.' The last time they had had words about her gambling she had packed her bags and left his house.

Her mouth twisted. She was so enraged he scarcely recognised her. 'I think that you forget that I have my own resources and my own estate in Northumbria. I will no longer reside with you. I shall leave tomorrow.'

This was the first he'd heard about any private income or an estate in Northumbria that wasn't under his control. 'You would leave without seeing your daughter married? Why should you punish Amanda for something that's not her fault?'

He'd hoped mentioning his forthcoming nuptials would be enough to defuse the situation but it had the reverse effect.

'You have control of my daughters and they care nought for my opinion nowadays. I shall take the travelling carriage . . .'

'I wasn't aware that you own a vehicle of that sort. Is this another secret you have been keeping from me?'

'Do you refuse to let me take the Sinclair carriage?'

'I do indeed. You will remain here until after the wedding and then I will make suitable arrangements for your journey. The name of this estate if you please?'

'Selby Manor, it is adjacent to Ouston Moor, some thirty miles from Newcastle. It was gifted to me by my grandmother.'

'Travelling that far will take a week or more and involve several overnight stops. I will send someone tomorrow and they can reserve your accommodation at suitable hostelries. They can also ensure that the house is fit for habitation. Is it occupied?'

He had deliberately kept his tone even and kept talking about details in the hope that she would recover her temper and change her mind. Alas, this was not the case.

'That is none of your concern. All you need to know, sir, is that you will regret sending me away. I intend to speak to Captain Marchand tomorrow on the subject of your man. You can be very sure the marshals will know exactly where to look.'

'You're prepared to cause the death of a good man in order to spite me? I cannot believe what I'm hearing. Sarah and Amanda will be horrified and you might well find yourself permanently estranged from them.'

'They have no need of me now. I have given the best part of my life to raising my children and in future I shall consider only what is best for me.' She swept past him, stalked through the doors and vanished upstairs.

He could see no way of preventing her from revealing the truth about Patrick. He must go at once to the Dower House and warn him to leave immediately.

'Richard, I heard raised voices and my mother almost pushed me down the stairs in her hurry to get past. Was she gambling again?'

'Unfortunately, my love, that was exactly what she was doing. Our guests refused to play and I went in to speak to her and mishandled it badly. She will reveal our secret tomorrow and is then determined to move to her own estate in Northumbria.'

'Don't look so perturbed, my dear, she'll calm down by the morning and all this will be forgotten. She has the most fearsome temper but when she recovers, she bears no grudges.'

'I sincerely hope you're right. Did you know that she had her own property and income?'

'I did not. I cannot think why she has never mentioned it to us as it would come to me on her death.'

'I think I will pre-empt her revelation and speak to Marchand myself. He's a reasonable fellow, maybe we can come to some arrangement.'

'Sarah's sleeping peacefully now, the laudanum has worked. Shall we take a stroll in the garden before we retire? I love to hear the nightingales singing.'

One of the things he adored about his beloved was that she couldn't give a fig if her slippers were ruined by the dew or if the hem of her gown became wet. She would have made an excellent officer's wife and been able to follow the drum in a way that few gently bred ladies could.

She had her skirt in one hand and the other was looped through his arm. It was cool outside and he guided her towards the steps that led into the rose garden. The heady perfume from the blooms drifted up to them and he was about to remark on it when two shapes loomed from the darkness.

'Tarnation take it, gentlemen, you startled us. I didn't know you were prowling about outside.'

'I beg your pardon, your grace, Lady Amanda. We thought to enjoy the nightingales before retiring.'

Richard laughed. 'I need to speak to you both and was in fact going to come in search of you later. There's a couple of stone benches over there we can use.' They immediately understood this was an order rather than a suggestion.

'I'll go in . . .'

'No, sweetheart, sit with me. There's nothing I can say or do that I don't wish you to know about.'

Her soft peal of laughter made him want to snatch her from the ground and make love to her.

'Good heavens, your grace, you've left yourself open to all sorts of complications once we are wed.'

He pulled her closer and kissed the top of her head hoping this wasn't seen in the dark. The moon was waning and only the reflected light from the candles still burning in the drawing room was providing illumination.

'I'm quite certain that you've guessed that Sergeant Major Riley is Mr Patrick O'Riley. He has left the neighbourhood and has no intention of returning until after his five years are up.'

'Thank you for being honest and saving us a deal of aggravation. I assume you have a proposition,' the captain replied.

'I do. I intend to write several letters, including one to Wellington himself. I would like you to deliver them for me. All the recipients are in Portugal which I'm sure is where you'd rather be.' This wasn't what he'd originally planned but he thought it a scheme more likely to succeed.

'And how will this be of benefit to us, your grace?'

'I intend to provide sufficient funds for both of you to transfer to an active regiment. My former brigade commander, Colonel Jackson, is always looking for likely officers and will take you on my recommendation.'

The young man didn't appear shocked at his blatant bribery. 'I take it that the other letters are to those in a position to stop the general from entrapping Riley.'

'I knew at once that you're an intelligent fellow. I suggest that you hang around here for a sennight. Send your private to London with a letter saying that you're hopeful of making an arrest. This will keep him out of the way for a week.'

'Excellent. Then Robinson and I can take a packet to Corunna and go in search of your commanding officer. I would have done it without the bribe, your grace, but I'm not going to refuse your offer of funds.'

'Good man. I warn you that you'll be accosted in the morning by the dowager as she and I are at daggers drawn.'

He stood up and drew Amanda with him. 'Come, my love, we'll continue our stroll. I bid you good night, gentlemen.'

'Your grace, is it possible that Lady Sarah will be able to join us before I depart? I would really like to apologise in person for causing her accident.'

'Don't be a dolt, sir. She followed *you*, and fell when you were nowhere near. It will be better if she remains where she is until we're certain of the extent of her injury. However, in a day or two I have no objection if you wish to visit her in her sitting room as long as Lady Amanda and Miss Westley are present.'

Amanda stiffened beside him and he knew she disapproved of his offer. She waited until they were away from the other two before expressing her displeasure.

'Have you run mad, Richard? My sister is halfway to falling in love with that man and the last thing she needs is to have him visit her. It will end in disaster.'

He silenced her with a kiss and a satisfactory few minutes later he raised his head. 'I think he would make an ideal husband for her. She would enjoy gallivanting across the Peninsula after him, don't you think?' He waited for the explosion trying hard not to laugh. As always, she surprised him.

'You're a nincompoop to think I would fall for that. I'm not remaining outside to bandy words with you, your grace. You can continue your walk on your own.'

She was several yards away before he reacted and he could hear her laughing in the darkness as she ran inside.

★ ★ ★

Sarah was carried gently to the daybed in her sitting room by Richard. 'You must give me your word that you'll not leave this bed unless it is to relieve yourself. I'll carry you to the commode.'

'You'll do no such thing. How can

you mention something so indelicate?' She was pink from toes to crown at his remark.

He grinned, quite unrepentant. 'I'm a rough soldier, remember, my dear. I've no regard for silly sensibilities. If you don't wish me to do it then I'll send up a footman.'

The idea of that was even worse. 'I can hop . . .'

'Dammit, Sarah, I don't think you understand the possible seriousness of your injury. If it's broken, and you wish to heal without permanent damage, you must remain where you are. I've sent for a physician from London that I know is competent. However, until he does come you will do as I say.'

'I promise. I'm sorry if I'm causing you unnecessary worry.'

He spun a chair and sat. 'I take it you haven't heard about your mother?'

She was aghast at his tale and he was surprised that Amanda hadn't already informed her of the drama. 'All this on top of your problems with Mr O'Riley. I

70

can only apologise again . . . '

'Nonsense, my dear. None of this is your fault — apart from hurting your ankle, of course.' He left the chair by the *chaise longue* and strolled out with a casual wave. He really was a most disturbing gentleman and she was glad that he was not going to be her husband.

Amanda arrived along with her breakfast tray. 'I gather that Richard has told you about the confrontation with Mama. Did he tell you that he's given the captain permission to visit later?'

'I don't wish to see him. It's hard to credit that our parent is prepared to abandon us because Richard won't allow her to gamble for money.'

'I'm hoping that she'll reconsider but even if she does, I've a nasty suspicion Richard won't forgive her so easily this time. By the way, did he tell you about his plans for the captain and Mr O'Riley?'

When her sister had finished explaining Sarah wasn't sure if she was concerned or impressed. 'All I can say is that I'm almost glad I'm confined to my apartment and not part of all this excitement. Please make sure that I have no unwanted visitors.'

'I'll do that. Mama can't depart until Richard has ensured her estate in Northumbria is fit for occupation. He's also having accommodation reserved for her long journey. I'm sure she'll be up to see you sometime today, or would you class her as an unwanted visitor too?'

'Certainly not. I was upset that she didn't visit last night. She's as contrary as a weathervane and I scarcely know who she is any more. I am sharp-set and that food set out on the table beside me is making my mouth water. Are you joining me or are you eating downstairs?'

* * *

The day dragged by and even a visit from her younger sibling, Beth, and Miss Westley did little to alleviate the boredom. Mama had yet to put in an appearance and she was beginning to think that her mother might well depart without speaking to her. Fortunately, she was only obliged to ask for Richard's assistance once during the day.

The following morning she was almost tempted to hop as her ankle scarcely hurt at all but decided against it. Then to her delight he appeared at the door of her bedchamber wheeling a somewhat dilapidated bath chair.

'Your carriage awaits, my lady. It might look ancient but it works perfectly well. I want to see if you can transfer yourself to it with your maid's assistance and without putting stress on your injury.'

She was fully dressed and lying on her bed as to do this hadn't involved putting her foot down. The peculiar contraption was a few inches lower than her bed but between Mary and herself they accomplished the task easily.

'Excellent. My services are no longer required. The doctor should be here later today and we'll know more then.' He paused at the door, his expression serious. 'Has your mother been to see you?'

'No, I do wish she would come as I might be able to persuade her to reconsider her decision.'

'I've not seen her since the other night as she's remained in her apartment and refuses to speak to either Amanda or me.'

'Then she didn't carry out her threat to reveal our secret?'

'She wrote a letter and had her companion deliver it.'

Sarah looked away not wishing him to see how this information distressed her. Richard would never forgive a betrayal of that magnitude and neither would her sister.

Then he was crouching down beside her. 'Sweetheart, don't cry. Whatever she does, whatever she says, she will always be your mother and because of that I'll always forgive her behaviour.'

'Thank you. I just wish I could be sure that Amanda will be as magnanimous as you.'

'Whatever her feelings she too would do nothing to cause you distress. Are you quite sure you don't want a visit from the dashing young captain? He's desperate to see for himself that you're in no pain.'

'If I didn't know you better, Richard, I would think that you were attempting to throw us together. I've no interest in him. I told you a few months ago that I've no intention of becoming romantically involved with any gentleman for a year or two.'

'I'm doing no such thing, my dear, I just thought seeing a different face might make the time go faster. I know how you hate to be cooped up inside.' He smiled down at her. 'A little light flirtation would take your mind off everything.'

'Flirting isn't a skill I have. I don't know how to do it. I'm not like my sister, who wore us to a frazzle by the time she was allowed on her feet after her riding accident three years ago, and my incarceration will not perturb me overmuch.'

Then she remembered something her mother had said and her spirits lifted a little. 'At least now I won't be obliged to fend off the unwanted suitors that my mother told me she has invited to your wedding.'

He said something extremely impolite. 'This is the first I've heard of it. I'll deal with it immediately. I give you my word you'll not be importuned at our wedding celebrations.'

★ ★ ★

Paul wasn't accustomed to idleness. He was a soldier and expected to be busy. The enlisted man had departed for London with the letter for Horse Guards so there was nothing more he could do until the duke gave him leave to head for Dover and catch a ship to Portugal.

His uniform was uncomfortably hot and he had nothing with which to replace it. He was wandering disconsolately around the garden when Lady Amanda appeared on the terrace and beckoned him over. He had no idea what had happened to Robinson as he hadn't seen him since they broke their fast an hour or so ago.

76

'Captain, you're approximately the same height and build as both this duke and the previous one.'

He nodded, uncertain as to why this information should be relevant to him.

'I've had a footman put out a selection of garments that I think will serve you well until you leave. Unfortunately, I've nothing that will fit your ensign so he'll have to suffer from the heat.'

'That's very thoughtful of you, my lady, but I'm obliged to remain in uniform however much I might wish to divest myself of this heavy jacket.'

'Fiddlesticks to that! Who is there here to see you? I've spoken to his grace and he was most insistent that you were comfortable. I think he has some tasks for you to do. Your arrival means that his man of business is necessarily elsewhere.'

Paul laughed. 'This is all highly irregular, but then so is what we've planned. Thank you, my lady, I should be delighted to change from my uniform and also to do anything I can to assist the duke.'

The breeches were slightly loose and

a trifle long but not enough to bother him. The shirts were by their very nature loose fitting so that was no problem at all. The three topcoats were a better fit as his shoulders were as broad as the original owner. The fact that the sleeves were, like the breeches, a bit long was no impediment.

He sent the liveried servants away as he had no use for a valet. He preferred to do for himself. When he strolled downstairs a while later, he was a new man, but was still unsure if he was breaking the rules of etiquette by wearing the clothes of a deceased duke.

'Excellent, they fit you almost as well as they did me. I abhor writing, my scrawl's almost indecipherable. Do you have a fair hand?'

'I do, your grace, I had it thrashed into me as a boy.'

'Then I'll dictate and you shall be my scribe. You need to know the content as although these will be delivered on my behalf, they also concern you.' The duke smiled. He was really a most charming man when he wasn't scowling or shouting. 'I've sent Robinson to the village on an errand for Lady Amanda. I think he was relieved to have something to do.'

'I'm certain that he was, your grace. Are you quite certain that you're comfortable with me wearing these garments?'

'When Amanda suggested that you borrow them, I agreed immediately. I don't stop for luncheon so I hope you ate sufficient at breakfast as you'll get nothing until we dine at six o'clock.'

They'd been working for an hour or two when there was a discreet knock at the door and the butler announced that the physician from London had arrived to examine Lady Sarah.

'I'll come at once. Have coffee and pastries brought here for the captain.'

Paul wandered about the study unable to settle until the duke returned and could tell him what the grand doctor's diagnosis was. He prayed it was merely a bad sprain and that the girl wouldn't be marooned upstairs unable to move because her ankle was broken.

A different footman arrived with the refreshments at the same time as his grace.

'Don't look so anxious, Marchand, the news is good. A severe sprain, the patient will be joining us for dinner tonight.'

'I cannot tell you how relieved I am that the injury is no worse.'

The remainder of the day was spent in a similar fashion. His hand was aching when eventually the duke patted him on the shoulder. 'Enough writing for today, my friend, we must adjourn and change for dinner. Tonight, Miss Westley will join us, again at Amanda's suggestion, so that our numbers will be even.'

5

Sarah paid particular attention to her appearance that evening. This was the first time they had entertained since they'd moved from the Dower House and she wanted to look her best.

'Amanda, I cannot wear a stocking or shoe on my injured ankle. Do I wear just one or none at all?'

'None at all. That gown is sufficiently long to cover your omission. Are you going to be carried and then travel in your bath chair or do you intend to hop?'

Richard spoke from behind them. He had a disconcerting habit of appearing when least expected. She supposed she should be grateful they were in the sitting room and not in her bedchamber.

'There's no need to do either of those things. Marchand has proved himself dextrous and made you a crutch so you can make your own way about the place.' He handed over the object and she was suitably impressed.

'It's the perfect length too. I'd better try it out before I decide.' She put it under her arm and was about to use it when her sister called her name in warning.

'Wait, you're going to ruin your gown. It's trapped beneath the end of the crutch.'

'Botheration! I don't see how I can overcome this difficulty. If I wear something shorter then my lack of stockings and shoes will be apparent.'

He vanished into Amanda's bedroom and returned with a piece of ribbon that almost matched her gown. 'Allow me, sweetheart, I'll shorten your skirt on this side.' Before she could protest, he was on his knees and fiddling about with her gown.

'Richard, desist. You're embarrassing my sister. Your solution might be ingenious but will not do. Sarah, I think you'll have to allow him to carry you and then use your chair.'

He had continued at her feet until he

was satisfied. Only then did he stand up. She looked down and thought his efforts quite ingenious. Her initial discomfort at having him so close seemed silly now.

'Thank you, that will do perfectly. I doubt that anyone will see my bare feet as long as I remember to keep my skirts in order when I'm seated.'

It took her a few attempts to master moving with the aid of a crutch but she was soon proficient enough for her companions to agree she was ready to descend.

'There's no need to hover so anxiously beside me, Richard, I'm not going to fall head first down the stairs I can assure you.'

'In which case, I'll walk in front then if you do stumble you won't go far.'

Miss Westley joined them. 'I'm so glad to see you mobile again, Lady Sarah. How long do you think you will be incapacitated?'

'Doctor Adams, the man who came from Town, assured me I should be good as new within the week as long as I keep my weight from it.'

Negotiating the curved staircase was slightly trickier than she'd anticipated but she managed it, albeit more slowly than she would have liked. As soon as she was in the hall Amanda and Richard left her to progress more slowly with Miss Westley at her side.

As the weather was clement the doors at the end of the drawing room were open and drinks were being served on the terrace. She viewed the length she had to traverse with disfavour.

'I think I'll remain inside. The thought of hopping all the way to the terrace and then back again when it's time to dine is just too much for me. Please, you go and join the others outside. I'm quite content to sit on my own.'

Miss Westley hesitated. 'Are you quite sure, my lady?'

'I am. Dinner will be served in half an hour and I'm happy to spend that short amount of time in my own company. Having been upstairs for two days, just being down is treat enough.'

She had barely settled when Captain Marchand appeared at her side. He had not come from the terrace but from behind her.

'Lady Sarah, do I have your permission to join you?'

'You do, captain. In fact you don't need anybody's permission to do anything in this establishment — my cousin stands on no ceremony and is the least toplofty duke you're likely to find anywhere.'

Only then did she notice he was no longer wearing his smart red uniform but dressed in what looked suspiciously like her papa's clothes. His smile, for some unaccountable reason, made her heart skip a beat.

'I know, reprehensible of me to appear in these when I should be in my regimentals. His grace insisted that I replace his man of business as it's entirely my fault — according to him — that he's been left to manage on his own.'

'I prefer you in civilian clothes, and from now on shall refer to you as Mr

Marchand as it will seem odd to use a military title.'

'Exactly so. I expect that you're aware of what his grace is organising on the behalf of myself and Mr Robinson?'

'My sister told me everything. I think it an excellent notion and will benefit all concerned.'

'I came expressly to apologise for my part in your accident. I cannot tell you how relieved I am that your injury is no more serious than a bad sprain.'

'The accident was entirely my doing, sir. You have nothing to apologise for. From the ink stains on your fingers I assume that you've been scribbling away all day. My cousin's handwriting is barely legible.'

'I have, my lady. Tomorrow I'm to accompany him to Ipswich on some legal matter or other. I sincerely hope that I'm not recognised out of uniform as I might well be cashiered if I was.'

'I rather think that having you as his secretary is somewhat worse than insisting that you remove your uniform.' No sooner had she said these words than she realised they could be misinterpreted. No well brought up lady would dream of mentioning anything so *risqué* as a gentleman removing his clothes.

Instead of being shocked by her immodest comment he laughed out loud. 'Worse than that, my lady, it was your sister that made the suggestion, not his grace.' He'd understood immediately her distress and put her at her ease.

'In which case, Mr Marchand, I'm going to suggest something even further from the pale than that.'

'I am agog, my lady, as to what that might be.' His eyes brimmed with amusement.

'I wish you to refer to me as Sarah, and I shall call you — I do not know your given name but would dearly like to use it. I cannot remain on formal terms with someone marching around in my departed papa's ensemble.'

'My name is Paul. I'd be honoured to address you so familiarly but I think it might be wise to speak to his grace . . . '

Yet again her cousin had arrived so quietly neither of them had been aware of his coming. 'Upon what subject do you wish to speak to me?' Richard's enquiry was bland but his expression was watchful.

'I have asked if we can ignore the rules and address each other as if we were friends. He to call me Sarah and I call him Paul. For some reason he thinks that your permission is needed before we do this.'

'He's quite correct to ask me. I should refuse but, as you so rightly pointed out, my dear, it's hard to remain on normal terms in the present circumstances so I've decided to give you my blessing. However, I suggest that you keep this informality between yourselves and don't involve the others.'

The look he gave Paul would have terrified a lesser man. 'I thank you, your grace, I can assure you that using our given names will be the only rule that we'll be breaking.'

Richard didn't suggest Paul addressed

him in any way but formally and this was noted by herself and her companion. His agreement was to indulge her, not to encourage Paul to take even the slightest liberty.

The two men nodded and then Richard was his usual relaxed persona once more. 'You cannot hide away in here, Sarah. Miss Westley says you believe it to be too far to walk so I've brought your carriage.' He gestured to the bath chair. This object, the last time she'd seen it, had been in her shared sitting room.

She pushed herself upright carefully keeping her weight off her damaged ankle and then dropped with more haste than dignity into the chair. She'd moved so swiftly as she feared that one or other of them would snatch her up and she'd no wish to be carried.

Unfortunately, the vehicle took off across the smooth carpet and only Paul's lightning reactions prevented another mishap. 'I believe that the old adage 'look before you leap' might be one you bear in mind in future.'

'Thank you once again for your intervention, Paul. Could I prevail upon you to wheel me outside to join the others?'

She bit her lip not sure if she was trying not to cry or laugh. Then she heard smothered sniggers from behind her — Richard was definitely finding the situation funny.

'I thank you not to poke fun at me, cousin, I can hear you quite well.' She twisted in the seat and fixed him with a frosty stare.

He shook his head. 'I'd no idea you were as amusing as your sister. You almost catapulted from that chair . . . ' He was unable to continue and no longer made any attempt to hide his laughter.

He was right — the situation was risible. By the time they reached the terrace all three of them were mopping their eyes and their laughter drew the others to the door to see what was causing so much merriment.

This was the perfect start to a quite delightful evening. For some reason champagne was served and she accepted a small glass although she rarely consumed anything alcoholic. Miss Westley conversed happily with Mr Robinson who was looking smart, but overheated, in his regimentals.

When dinner was announced they moved as one towards the dining room. A slight sound above her made her look up. She caught a glimpse of her mother — it was like looking at a stranger. Her stomach clenched and her appetite deserted her.

She was being pushed at the rear of the party by Paul. He looked at her. 'What's wrong? Are you feeling unwell?'

'I am. I should not have had the champagne it doesn't agree with me. I must return to my apartment.'

'It will be quicker if I carry you.' He reached down and scooped her into his arms. She rested her head against his shoulder hoping that neither Richard nor Sarah came out to investigate before she was safely in her bedchamber. Her crutch had been left in the bath chair.

Her maid was absent as she wouldn't

have expected her to return so soon. 'Thank you, Paul, if you would be kind enough to put me on the *chaise longue* and then send a servant up with my crutch, I should be most grateful.'

'I'll do that. I sincerely hope that you feel well enough to join us tomorrow.'

She leaned back and closed her eyes trying to push the image of Mama from her mind. To be stared at with such hate by one's own parent was not something she'd ever thought to experience.

The door opened but she didn't look up. 'Put my crutch beside me. I don't require anything else.'

* * *

Paul decided it would be simpler for him to return the forgotten item himself. He picked it up, was about to leave, but then decided it would be sensible to let the other diners know what was happening.

The duke was on his way to investigate as Paul stepped in. 'Lady Sarah was feeling unwell. She believes the champagne has upset her digestion. I carried her to her apartment and am now taking up her crutch. I'll join you in a few minutes.'

'We were concerned when you didn't appear. Alcohol does disagree with her; I should not have allowed her to drink it.'

Her sister, who had been rising to her feet, settled back in her chair with a smile. 'Don't be long, Mr Marchand, as the food is about to be served.'

The sitting room door had been open when he'd left a few moments ago and now it was closed. Sarah couldn't have done it. Who the hell was in there with her? He didn't hesitate. He didn't knock. He quietly opened the door and stepped through.

In two strides he was across the room and threw his arms around the woman who had hold of Sarah by the shoulders. 'No, your grace, that will not do.' He stepped back using his considerable weight to break her grip.

'How dare you put your hands on me. You insolent creature. I'll have you horsewhipped.'

'Your grace, I think it would be best if you return to your apartment until you have recovered your composure.' He kept his words even, spoke calmly, but it was taking every ounce of his strength to hold her. He backed towards the door praying that she wouldn't start screaming.

Sarah was ashen-faced. Her eyes wide — seemingly unable to speak so distressed was she by this unprovoked attack from her mother.

Then the duke was at his side and stepped between the dowager and her daughter. The struggling ceased.

'Madam, if you continue in this manner, I'll have you locked in a lunatic asylum. Is that what you want?' He spoke so quietly Sarah could not have heard his threat but it did the trick.

His burden sagged against him and he was obliged to support her rather than restrain her. He was about to explain when the duke shook his head.

'Not here, let me take her. You go to Sarah.'

'Come along, your grace, you will be more comfortable elsewhere.'

Paul relinquished his hold and stepped aside. What the hell was going on here? He'd come to arrest an innocent man as a traitor and was now up to his neck in some other drama. He'd made enquiries about this family before setting out for Suffolk and no one had mentioned that the Dowager Duchess was mentally unstable.

'Paul, thank you for coming. We don't know why she attacked me. I think she's lost her mind.'

'Let me see, did she hurt you?' He pointed to her shoulders. She shook her head and brushed away her tears.

'A few bruises, nothing serious. I don't understand why she would do that to me. She's never raised a hand to any of us before this. In fact, we were never physically chastised by either parent as they didn't believe in punishments of that sort.'

He was relieved that she sounded composed. 'If this behaviour is so out of character then there must be something physical that's causing this aberration. I've seen men run mad from fever, and once after being bitten by a rabid dog.'

'We have no dogs here, but my younger sister, Beth, suffered from inflammation of the brain and has forever remained a child of six in her abilities. I pray that my mother hasn't contracted something similar. I can think of no other reason why she should have come in here and tried to hurt me.'

They were interrupted by the sudden arrival of both Miss Westley and Lady Amanda. 'Surely I didn't hear aright? Tell me at once what happened and why Mr Marchand and Richard have abandoned us to our own devices downstairs.'

Paul left Sarah to explain. He and Robinson shouldn't be here witnessing this family catastrophe. They would remove themselves at once to the inn in the village where they had reserved rooms on their arrival two days ago.

He met his ensign wandering about outside the dining room. He quickly explained what had transpired. 'I'll get the horses saddled, sir, whilst you change back into your uniform. My belongings are still inside my pack so if you would be so kind as to collect them you can leave as soon as you come down.'

Before they could move there was a flurry of movement and the duke, Lady Amanda and Miss Westley hurried towards them.

'Dinner is congealing on the table, my friends, shall we set to before it is completely ruined?' His grace gripped him firmly by the elbow and he found himself in the dining room whether he wanted to be there or not.

'Your grace, I think it would be best if we left. I can assure you that . . . '

'Mr Marchand, my mother is temporarily unwell. My sister is unharmed and there's absolutely no need for you to do anything apart from enjoy your dinner.' Lady Amanda's smile appeared genuine.

If the family were unperturbed by the extraordinary behaviour of the dowager then he would follow their lead and pretend everything was as it should be.

There were three courses with several removes and all of it, no doubt, perfectly cooked and quite delicious but he tasted none of it. Wine was offered but he refused as did the others. Conversation was somewhat stilted and he was relieved when her ladyship put down her napkin and stood up.

He expected that Robinson and himself would remain behind with the duke but this wasn't to be the case. He tossed his damask square aside and pushed his chair back.

'Can I ask you to play for us, my love?'

'I should love to, but first I will run up and see that Sarah is well.'

'I am perfectly well, thank you for asking, dearest sister. As you see, I have made my way unaided to join you for the remainder of the evening. Listening to you play is exactly what I'd like.'

Sarah was looking pale but as beautiful as ever. He hesitated not sure if he had the right to go to her side and offer his assistance. He was glad that he had done so as the duke strode across.

'You should have asked for your chair to have been brought. Did you eat anything?'

'I'll have something later, Richard, and I've become an expert with my crutch and had no difficulty at all descending the stairs safely.'

Paul had noticed the splendid piano halfway down the drawing room and had wondered who amongst the girls was proficient on the instrument. He sat with Robinson, Miss Westley sat with Sarah and the duke sprawled on a chair that didn't seem sturdy enough to bear his weight.

Then Amanda began to play and he knew at once he was in the presence of a truly great pianist. Her fingers flew across the keys — she played from memory — and within minutes the audience was entranced.

When the impromptu concert ended, he applauded enthusiastically. The atmosphere was different now, less strained, more relaxed. When the supper tray was wheeled in later he was pleased to see

Sarah eating hungrily.

He nodded to his junior officer and he got the message. It was time for them to retire and leave the family to discuss private matters without them present. Miss Westley followed them out.

6

Richard had been able to push the difficulty of his future mother-in-law's behaviour to one side whilst Amanda was playing but now they were alone he needed to address the problem.

'Sarah, what exactly did your mother say to you?'

She was unsurprised by his question and had obviously been expecting to be asked what had happened earlier. He'd understood immediately that this was the reason she'd made the effort to join them.

'She said nothing at all. She just rushed across the room and started shaking me. She was like a madwoman — not someone I recognised. Do you think she might have contracted the fever that so damaged dear Beth's brain?'

'I don't think so, sweetheart, she has no fever or any other signs of illness. Amanda, my love, do you have any suggestions as to why your mother behaved this way?'

'She has always had an unpredictable temperament but never has she acted in such a fashion. It's hard to credit that she has lost her mind simply because you've forbidden her to gamble. However, everything points to that being the answer.'

He had a nasty suspicion his beloved might well be right. 'I've sent for a doctor from Ipswich who, so I've been told, is a forward thinker and has written papers about mental derangement. Doctor Peterson should be here first thing tomorrow morning.' He looked from one to the other of the girls reluctant to tell them what he felt obliged to put in place with regard to their parent.

Amanda sensed at once that something was wrong. 'Tell us, Richard, whatever you've done we will support you.'

'I've had the external doors to your mother's apartment locked. She now has her personal maid plus one other to take care of her. Until we know the extent of her confusion I believe that I've no choice but to confine her.'

'I was going to suggest that you did so, my dear, because next time she might do one of us some serious harm in her madness. Imagine how frightened Beth would be if . . .'

There wasn't any necessity for Amanda to finish her sentence. Both he and Sarah knew to what she was referring.

'I hate to say this, darling girl, but I fear we must postpone our nuptials until your mother is better.'

Sarah shook her head. 'You must do no such thing. Why not cancel the wedding breakfast and celebration ball and just marry in a simple ceremony with only family present?'

He was about to refuse when Amanda jumped to her feet and threw her arms around her sister. 'That's an excellent suggestion, dearest, and to be honest I would much prefer something small and private.' She turned and looked at him enquiringly. 'What do you think? Would Sarah's suggestion be acceptable to you?'

He could hardly say to either of them

that he didn't give a damn how they got married as long their vows were exchanged at the earliest opportunity.

'It would suit me perfectly. Like you, I'm uncomfortable in a crowd. As our banns have already been read, we could marry tomorrow if you wish? Marchand can act as my groomsman and witness and Robinson will do for the other one.'

He waited for Amanda to protest at his high-handed suggestion but her smile was radiant. 'As we intended to marry in the family chapel anyway all we need to do is contact the vicar.'

'It's fortunate our chapel hasn't been demolished like the house. If you and Sarah make the necessary arrangements for flowers and so on, then I'll do the rest. Are you content to marry so swiftly whatever the outcome of the visit from the doctor, sweetheart?'

'I am. There's little to do for such a small ceremony. I already have my wedding gown in my closet. I just need to speak to the housekeeper about suitable refreshments for afterwards. Richard, has Mr O'Riley really gone to Scotland?'

'No, I sent him to Northumbria on your mother's behalf. He will be absent for a month.'

'He could hardly attend your wedding, sister, when the two officers who have come to arrest him are residing here.'

Sarah had taken his comment at face value but Amanda knew him better and raised an eyebrow. He nodded to indicate that she was correct in her assumption that Patrick was still in the neighbourhood.

'I hardly think our new friends would do any such thing, Sarah. After all, the pretence that Sergeant Major Riley is not in fact Mr O'Riley hasn't been questioned by staff or neighbours so far. I don't see why this couldn't be allowed to continue.'

'The question's academic, my love, as he's already elsewhere. Do you require my assistance to return to your chamber, Sarah?'

She saw her hesitate and realised she was dreading having to make the return journey. Amanda was before him. 'I shall fetch your carriage, my love, and then Richard can carry you up the stairs. It's been an interesting day but not an enjoyable one.'

He followed her out and pulled her into his arms. 'As far as I'm concerned your mother can run mad as often as she wishes as it now means I can take you to my bed tomorrow night.'

She pressed herself against him for a second and then stepped away. 'You are too eager, sir, and I've no intention of pre-empting my wedding vows.' Her eyes were sparkling, her cheeks flushed and it took all his willpower to let her go.

* * *

Seeing Amanda so happy to be marrying Richard made Sarah reconsider her determination to remain single until she was one and twenty. This was to be the last night that she would share an apartment with her sister. Tomorrow everything would change. There would be a new Duchess of Denchester and she would have a new brother who was also her guardian and a very distant cousin.

She refused to be downhearted at the thought of losing her sister. Whatever was said to the contrary once the knot was tied Amanda wouldn't have the time to spend with her or Beth. In future her attention must be on her husband. Good heavens — there might be a baby in the family next spring!

She was woken the following morning by Amanda calling her name. 'Sarah, I'm sorry to rouse you so early but I have the most dreadful news.'

'What is it? What has our mother done now?'

'She has gone. It seems her influence over those that have worked for her for years was greater than either Richard or I realised. Somehow, she persuaded her maids to pack her trunks and then for two footmen to carry them to the travelling carriage. And, even worse, she has taken a coachman and three grooms with her.'

'Has Richard gone after her?'

'He has — and he's taken Mr Marchand and Mr Robinson with him. I've never seen him so incensed. This will end badly for all of us.' Her sister flopped onto the end of the bed. Sarah had never seen her so disturbed. 'Today was supposed to have been my wedding day. God knows when that will take place now.'

'What time did Mama leave, do you know?'

'Sometime after midnight, which gives her five hours start.' Her sister rallied a little. 'The gentlemen will travel at twice the speed on horseback than she can do in a carriage. They might well overtake her by lunchtime and have her back by this evening.' Amanda jumped up her normal buoyant temperament restored.

'Is there anything I can do?'

'I'll help you dress as it's too early to call for Mary. Then you can write the letter to the vicar instead of Richard and arrange for the ceremony to take place tomorrow morning at eleven o'clock in the family chapel.'

'What if they aren't back by then?'

'Tell him it could be any time from eleven o'clock onwards and to be ready to perform the ceremony when called upon.'

Sarah thought it quite likely the ceremony would have to be postponed for more than a few hours but thought it better not to mention it. 'I'll also speak to Miss Westley and Beth later and make sure that they have their ensembles ready for your wedding.'

'I think it would be splendid if there were flowers in the chapel, don't you?'

'I do indeed. The gardens are full of summer blooms. I'll arrange for vases to be placed in the dining room as well. I think that the best room for your wedding breakfast.'

'Thank you, dearest, then all I have to do is speak to the housekeeper about the food.' She paused as she was dropping a pretty blue sprigged muslin over Sarah's head. 'What about our mother? She can hardly come back here — do you really think that Richard will incarcerate her in an asylum?'

'More to the point, is the fact that staff here have shown disloyalty to him. I think it likely he will dismiss them — and I wouldn't blame him at all.'

'I should have known her influence was far greater than mine. How could I have been so blind to the true state of affairs?'

Sarah grabbed her crutch and stood up. 'There, that will have to do. My hair can remain in its night-time braid until Mary comes. Are there many people working here who have been recently appointed?'

'To be honest, I've never given the matter any consideration. These details will be recorded in the accounts books. We must look through them immediately. Those that have worked for the family for less than five years, I think, could be considered loyal to the new regime.'

'And the others? Do you intend to get rid of all of them?'

'That will be for Richard to decide. Until I'm actually his duchess I have no true authority in this matter.'

The house was strangely quiet, no appetising aroma of breakfast drifting into the hall, and her stomach gurgled loudly.

'Do you need your chair or can you hop your way to the study?'

'I'm getting more proficient with this thing and can move about quite easily now. Where are you going?'

'I'll head for the kitchen and see if I can find us something to eat. If the range is hot enough, I'll make a pot of coffee as well.'

After a considerable time Sarah had already discovered a dozen staff who had joined the family within the last five years. There were still three more books to peruse. Why was Amanda taking so long to fetch coffee and cake? She glanced at the overmantel clock and confirmed it had been more than an hour.

With a sigh she pushed herself upright and put the crutch under her arm. There was no alternative but for her to go in search of her sister. On stepping out of the study she was aware the house had come alive whilst she'd been busy.

There were half a dozen maids on their knees scrubbing the floors, sacks tied around their waists to keep their smart blue gowns clean. If they were surprised to see her so early, they didn't show it.

'Good morning, my lady, we won't be long. Take care as the floor is wet,' one of the girls said cheerily.

'Thank you for the warning, Eliza, isn't it?' The girl nodded pleased her name had been remembered. 'Do you happen to know the whereabouts of Lady Amanda? She went to the kitchens over an hour ago and hasn't returned.'

'She weren't there when we was getting our water, my lady.'

This was very peculiar — yet another thing to worry about. She was concerned about Richard's possible actions when he caught up with Mama. He was a fierce and formidable gentleman when angry and she wouldn't like to be on the receiving end of his rage.

The doctor! Good heavens, they'd

both quite forgotten this man was coming to examine her mother and she was no longer here. As she didn't know the address of this gentleman she couldn't cancel the appointment.

When she emerged into the hall she heard voices in the drawing room. One of them she recognised as her sister's, but the other, a deep masculine one, she was unfamiliar with. It was only five o'clock in the morning — who could be visiting at this time?

★　★　★

Paul had scarcely had time to change back into his uniform before setting out with the duke to find the missing dowager.

'Sir, do you think we should be participating in this escapade?' Robinson asked as he was hastily buckling up the girth of his mount.

'As we're going in the direction of the missing Riley then I think there'll be no problem with Horse Guards.'

'Fair enough, I'm game. There's nothing I like more than galloping about the countryside in the middle of the night.'

Paul wasn't sure if his companion was being sarcastic or actually enjoyed travelling at speed in pitch darkness with a high risk of breaking his neck.

The duke yelled from the stable yard. 'At the double, if you please. We need to depart now, not next week.'

He led his horse out and mounted smoothly as did Robinson. It would seem they were not even to carry lanterns on poles but rely entirely on the inadequate light of the moon. Their saddlebags were already strapped to their saddles. Only the barest necessities for an overnight stay — but enough to ensure they could remain respectable despite their long ride.

'Your grace, are we the only ones in pursuit? You're taking no grooms?'

'I think the three of us are more than adequate for the task of capturing one elderly, unstable old lady.' His laughter echoed in the darkness. This gentleman was certainly a very odd duke.

To make matters more interesting his grace decided to travel across country. This made sense as it would halve the journey time, but thundering across fields and jumping ditches and hedges without being able to see where one was going was a recipe for catastrophe.

However, the leader of their small band knew exactly what he was doing and as long as they followed his lead they were in no real danger. After half an hour he began to enjoy this wild ride despite the fact that they'd brought only a clean shirt and stock and were going to be unpleasantly hot and sweaty by the time they reached their quarry.

After the initial gallop they were now travelling at a collected canter — safer and kinder to their horses. After two hours their pace slowed to a walk to allow the animals to cool down and recover.

'We can't be far behind them now, Marchand. There's a river, not deep, that we need to ford and our mounts can drink before we continue.' There was no need to answer, Paul indicated his having heard by raising his hand.

The only sound in the darkness was the jingling of bits and the soft pad of hoofs on the grass. Occasionally he heard the bark of a fox, a rustle in the undergrowth of nocturnal animals, and in the distance the sweet song of a nightingale. A perfect summer's night and he decided that after all he was happy to be part of this.

How many more perfect English evenings would he experience? Once he was fighting for King and Country the risk of dying or being seriously injured in battle was high. A captain led his men from the front, and an officer, if the enemy was clever, was always targeted first.

His sombre thoughts were interrupted when his horse increased his pace — the beast must have smelt water ahead. On reaching the riverbank he dismounted, as did the other two, pulled the reins over the animal's ears and then allowed him to drink his fill.

'I'm going to walk beside him for a

mile or two, your grace, he's blowing hard and needs the rest.'

'My stallion's not in so bad a case but he too will be better not having me on his back for a while.'

They waded through the shallow water and walked in single file down the well-trodden track, the duke, as before, in the lead. God knows how he recognised his surroundings so far from his own demesne. The fact that there was now the faintest glimmer of dawn on the horizon must make it easier to know in what direction one was going.

His gelding nudged him in the back almost making him miss his step. He reached up and stroked the velvety nose. 'What ails you, old friend? Have you heard something that we haven't?' He'd spoken quietly but the man in front had heard him and raised his hand to indicate they halt.

At first Paul heard nothing untoward but then there was a definite sound of voices somewhere to the left of them. To his surprise the duke dropped his reins and then vanished up a tree with the dexterity and speed of a small boy.

He landed with a thump beside them a few moments later. 'Nothing to worry about, it's a Romany camp. Your horse has sharp ears, my friend, you'll find that useful in Portugal.'

'Jacko and I have been together for several years. I broke him in myself. He's cool now, shall we remount?'

He heard a distant church clock chime and counted the strokes. Four o'clock — it would soon be full light and they could make more rapid progress. His lips curved. He doubted they could have travelled any faster in broad daylight.

As they cantered easily across the open field he drew alongside the duke. 'We must be ahead of them now, your grace. Do you have any notion where they might stop to rest the team and take refreshments?'

'The Coach and Horses is where we're headed. It's, as you might imagine, the place where the mail and stagecoaches

118

change teams. It's a substantial hostelry and exactly the sort of place that her grace would like.'

'Forgive me for asking, sir, but how do you intend to persuade her to return?'

'I don't intend to ask her opinion on the matter, she will do as she's bid. What I haven't decided is exactly where to put her.'

Paul wasn't sure if he was required to answer or if this was a rhetorical statement. The duke looked at him definitely waiting for a response.

'I know it's unpleasant at the moment with the building of your new home taking place only a few hundred yards away, but her grace can be kept safe at the Dower House as long as you have staff who are loyal to you taking care of her.'

'I thought that the best solution myself but I find that I no longer think with the military precision I once did and thank you for your opinion.'

'There is one possible problem, your grace. If your man of affairs is staying at this inn then I've no option but to arrest him.'

'In which case, I suggest that you allow me to ride ahead and thus avoid any embarrassing confrontations.' He put his stallion into a gallop and was soon out of sight.

'Are we to follow our noses, captain? The directions to this Coach and Horses are somewhat sketchy,' Robinson said with a grin.

'If you stand in your stirrups you can see a small town ahead. I hardly think it's going to be taxing to find this place. I believe I can hear the sound of the coach horn coming from that direction.'

7

Richard was glad to finish the journey on his own. He was no longer a hardened soldier and had found this midnight excursion more tiring than he'd expected. The past months had made him soft and in future he would take more exercise, sleep less and eat more frugally.

If anyone saw him smiling, they would think him fit for Bedlam. The thought of how he could ensure he was sleeping less was by spending the nights making love to Amanda. They were supposed to be getting married today but obviously that wasn't going to happen. God willing — they would tie the knot tomorrow.

He clattered into the yard and an obsequious ostler touched his forelock and took his reins. It could only be the magnificence of his stallion that had elicited this response as he certainly didn't look like anyone important.

He dropped to the floor and tossed

the waiting man his reins. 'Take care of him, brush him down thoroughly and feed him well.' The groom bowed and prepared to lead Othello into the stable block. 'A minute — do you have the Denchester travelling carriage and a team of matching bays here?'

'No, my lord, we ain't got nothing so grand at the moment.'

As there were no other establishments of this size and splendour in the town, he was certain this was where the dowager would halt. It would be easier for him to look in the stables to see if Patrick's horse was there, rather than draw attention to the fact that he was looking for him.

There were two dozen stalls, half of them occupied, and none of them with the horse which he was seeking. That was one less thing to worry about. He'd no wish to make life difficult for the young captain as he was coming to like him well enough. He rather thought that he wouldn't be the only one sad when the two provost marshals departed for the continent.

When he joked to Amanda about Sarah marrying Marchand, he hadn't for one minute believed they might form an attachment. Whatever his ward's feelings, he was certain that Marchand's were engaged.

The interior of the building was as well-maintained and clean as the stable block. The landlord was on duty despite the early hour and approached him and bowed. 'How can I be of service, sir? Are you desirous of a chamber or perhaps to break your fast?'

'I am the Duke of Denchester. I require two chambers, one for myself and one for my two companions who will be arriving at any moment. I doubt that we'll be staying overnight. We shall need to eat, but in a private parlour not in the common snug.'

'There will be hot water sent up immediately, your grace. I will have a private dining room prepared for you.' The man hesitated obviously not liking to ask exactly what was his illustrious guest's business.

'I wish to take you into my confidence.' He stared at the man and he nodded vigorously.

'You can rely on my discretion and also that of my staff.'

'Excellent. The Dowager Duchess of Denchester will be arriving in my carriage sometime this morning. I am here to take her home.'

The man's eyes widened as he took in the full meaning of this concise sentence. 'I understand perfectly, your grace. When her grace and her party arrive I shall ensure that they are given rooms in which she will be undisturbed.'

Richard nodded. 'Good. If she turns up whilst I'm upstairs you will not, of course, inform her of my presence.'

He strode back into the inn yard in order to speak to his companions who had just arrived. Their regimentals were attracting a deal of attention and he cursed under his breath. It would have been better if they had travelled incognito as it was quite possible one of the grooms might let slip that two soldiers were in residence. If this happened the carriage could travel straight on and he would be obliged to go after her again.

'We're in advance of them. There's a chamber reserved for you. Sort yourselves out and then make your way to the private parlour where a meal will be served.' He looked directly at the captain. 'My man of business is not here and hasn't been seen in this vicinity.'

'Thank you for the information, your grace.'

* * *

Richard stripped off his topcoat and shirt and plunged his head into the china basin into which he'd poured a generous amount of hot water. He then washed the sweat and grime from his upper body and, when dry, put on his clean shirt. He tied his stock in the simplest arrangement he knew, ran his fingers through his wet hair and put his freshly sponged jacket back on. A nervous maidservant had completed this task for him whilst he was about his ablutions.

Satisfied he looked respectable he gave his dusty boots a cursory wipe with a damp cloth and then was ready to descend. He pulled out his pocket watch and flicked it open. Six o'clock — the carriage would have been trundling along the roads for several hours and the occupants would be more than ready to relieve themselves and find refreshments. The team of horses pulling the vehicle would also be in dire need of food, water and rest.

They could not begin the return journey until early afternoon so there was ample time to eat and to snatch a few hours' sleep. Even if the dowager discovered he was here there was little she could do about it as the horses would be too fatigued to continue without several hours' respite.

The landlord was downstairs waiting to escort him with due ceremony to the room set aside for their personal occupancy.

'Your grace, I took the liberty of sending out a groom to enquire if those that you seek might have already passed through.'

Richard wasn't sure if he was irritated or impressed by this man's actions. 'I thank you.' He raised an eyebrow and waited to be told what had been discovered.

'The carriage that you seek hasn't arrived in this neighbourhood. However, young Seth said he's pretty sure it's about a mile away and should arrive in the next half an hour.'

He was about to say that it shouldn't take any carriage so long to cover so short a distance but then understood the significance. 'I take it the team is done and they are travelling at snail's pace.'

'Worse than that, your grace, the lead horse is lame. Do you wish me to send for the farrier?'

He nodded. 'Yes, do that. What is the coachman thinking to continue when one of the team is unsound?' This question was rhetorical and the landlord had

the sense not to do more than nod sym-
pathetically.

'We shall require the rooms overnight
after all. Will that be a problem?'

'No, your grace, I have already made
suitable adjustments to my books in
order to accommodate everyone. Seth
tells me there are two coachmen and
three outriders — how many passengers
are there apart from her grace?'

'Two maids have accompanied her.
They can share her accommodation. The
coachmen and grooms can doss down
wherever you like. At least one of their
mounts also goes under harness, so with
luck we can set out sometime tomorrow
morning.'

'I assume, your grace, that her grace
will wish to remain in her apartment
until you depart tomorrow?'

Richard was warming to this fellow
who understood the situation perfectly.
'Your assumptions are correct.' He nodded towards the narrow passageway on
the left. 'Have my travelling companions
descended before me?'

128

'The two officers are awaiting your arrival. Allow me to conduct you to them.'

* * *

The food served was excellent — but hardly surprising in such a superior establishment. Richard put down his cutlery with a sigh of satisfaction.

'I think it fortunate, gentlemen, that we arrived when we did. For I doubt that we'll get much more opportunity to sit and enjoy a repast without interruptions.'

'What do you wish us to do for you?'

'Your presence, fully armed, in uniform is enough to ensure the cooperation of the men who accompanied her grace. I intend to dismiss them without reference. They'll remain here when we return and be obliged to find their own way home.'

From the disapproving glance the two young men exchanged he realised they'd misunderstood him. 'Devil take it! I don't intend to leave them destitute. I'll give them sufficient to buy a seat on a common stage and, on their return, they can apply to the factor for any back wages they might be owed.'

How they were to arrange the return of the spare horses he'd yet to decide. Time enough for that when he'd spoken to her grace. God knows how she was going to react to his unexpected appearance.

★ ★ ★

Sarah almost pitched onto her nose in her effort to discover who had arrived at the house so early and was now entertaining her sister in the drawing room.

'Sarah, I do apologise for abandoning you in the study. I saw Doctor Peterson ride down the drive and so felt obliged to invite him in.'

The physician was of middle years, fiery red hair, and a friendly smile. He was on his feet and bowed to her.

'Lady Sarah, it is I who should apologise. I was attending someone in the neighbourhood and it hardly seemed worthwhile to go home and then return an hour or two later. I intended to put my horse in the stables and then find a quiet corner to doze until I could appear at your door.'

'Although the doctor's visit is no longer required, I insisted he came in for refreshments before returning to Ipswich,' Amanda said. 'He has been most magnanimous about the wasted journey.'

'Forgive me if this might seem an intrusion on your worries, my ladies, but my curiosity is aroused. Would you indulge me by answering some questions about your missing parent?'

'I think it unsuitable for us to remain in here unchaperoned, sir,' she replied.

'I shall go at once. I apologise for a second time for intruding.'

'No, sir, that's not what I meant. You are a most welcome, if somewhat early, visitor. My sister and I will go elsewhere until Miss Westley can join us and then no breach of etiquette will occur.'

Amanda was on her feet and nodded. 'Thank you for reminding me, dearest sister. I believe that I considered myself exempt from that rule as I am to become the wife of the Duke of Denchester tomorrow morning.'

The doctor bowed. 'Congratulations on your forthcoming nuptials, my lady. I am *de trop*.'

'I insist that you remain here and allow your horse to recover.' Amanda looked towards the door. 'Good, I can hear your breakfast arriving. We shall rejoin you in an hour or so — unless, of course, you decide to leave before then.'

Once across the hall Sarah spoke. 'Who did you find to make him anything at this hour?'

'There were two kitchen maids down to get the range heated and they said they could coddle eggs, slice ham and make toast and tea. No doubt Doctor Peterson will be somewhat startled to have his breakfast brought to him by them instead of footmen, but he doesn't seem the sort of gentleman to be upset by such informality.'

Sarah refused her sister's offer of help as she was now efficient on her crutch. 'I'm only halfway through the ledgers. If you assist me, I believe we can complete our task in another hour.'

'Have you compiled any sort of list? How many are there in Richard's employ?'

'We have, if you count indoor and outdoor staff, almost one hundred men, women, and some so young in years they could be considered little more than children. Amongst those I've so far managed to discover only twenty inside and fifteen outside servants who've not worked here for decades.'

When they reached the study Amanda yanked on the strap. The hour was early, but there should be more people awake and ready to come to their bidding.

'Whatever we might feel about those that disobeyed Richard and helped our mother to escape, if anyone has been working for the family for most of their adult lives they can hardly be dismissed without reference or pension.'

'He's a fair man. I think he'll give them the opportunity to pledge their allegiance to him before he sends them away.'

There was a hesitant knock on the door and her sister hurried to open it. A somewhat dishevelled footman, his half-wig askew and two buttons of his gold frogged livery undone, bowed deeply.

'I apologise for the delay, my lady. We didn't know you were downstairs so early.'

'We would like our breakfast served here as soon as maybe. Our unexpected guest has been served by the girls from the kitchen.'

The young man caught a glimpse of his disarray and hastily straightened his wig before backing out. From the racket he made he was running to attend to their requests.

Two trays arrived in short time and no further conversation was possible whilst they ate. A footman had been tasked with rousing Miss Westley and asking her to join them in the drawing room at her earliest convenience.

At eight o'clock Sarah shook out her skirts and was ready to depart. 'Are you going to speak to those who we believe will be loyal to us or will you wait until Richard returns?'

'As I said before, until I'm actually married to him, I've no real authority to deal with such matters. Goodness me! We should have asked Miss Westley to come to the study; she will be dismayed to find a strange gentleman in the drawing room instead of us.'

They arrived at the door to find the doctor and Miss Westley chatting happily, neither of them at all bothered about the somewhat unusual situation. Their former governess stood up and dipped politely.

'Good morning, I was about to come in search of you. Doctor Peterson and I introduced ourselves and I sent for more toast and coffee. This is a most unusual day.'

Only then did Sarah realise Miss

Westley would only just have discovered about Mama.

'Indeed it is, and tomorrow will be even more extraordinary,' Amanda said and then explained to Miss Westley that the wedding had been brought forward.

The doctor, rather than looking uncomfortable at being involved in such an intimate family conversation appeared to revel in it. 'I thought I had an exciting life when viewed from most people's viewpoint. However, I must own that this family's adventures quite trump my own.'

The coffee was brought in and conversation halted until the footman had departed. As Sarah's ankle was still too tender to stand on it fell to Miss Westley to pour coffee from the heavy, silver jug into the delicate porcelain cups.

The doctor immediately stood up and offered to assist and his kindness was immediately accepted. Once they were comfortably settled with the dark, aromatic brew and a selection of freshly baked biscuits the conversation turned to the reason that their visitor had volunteered to remain.

Amanda told him everything she could remember about their mother's volatile temperament and how in the past year, since Richard had arrived, her behaviour had worsened considerably. He listened quietly and attentively.

'I think there are two things at work here. The first is that her grace is at the time of life when ladies often suffer from emotional upset, irritation and other symptoms upon which I will not dwell. The second is a somewhat controversial diagnosis.' He stopped as if thinking they wouldn't wish to hear anything out of the ordinary.

'Please, sir, I am agog to hear what you're thinking however controversial it might seem,' Amanda said eagerly.

'I think the fact that the new Duke of Denchester is a pattern copy of the old one whilst only being a very remote connection might well have upset her grace. The fact that he wore her deceased husband's clothes for a while must also have been an added strain to her.'

'Forgive me, but I don't think that can be anything to do with it. Our parents lived separate lives for the past two decades because of his infidelities and there was no love left between them,' her sister said firmly.

'I agree, Amanda, I don't think it has anything to do with Richard's uncanny likeness to yourself and to our papa.'

The doctor smiled and nodded as if agreeing with their statements. 'These feelings can often be deep-seated in the mind. Her grace might well not be aware of them herself. What you tell me about their relationship just confirms my opinion.

'Imagine how difficult it must be for her to be constantly reminded of the gentleman she had once loved but who had betrayed her. At the same time his appearance will also make her recall the way things were before he died.'

'Good heavens! Now that you've explained it so well, I begin to think that you might have found the explanation,'

Sarah said.

Amanda wasn't so easily convinced. 'I think that some of her extreme behaviour could be due to the things that you mention. However, her addiction to gambling for high stakes is what has caused this particular aberration. She has never liked to be gainsaid and Richard stopping her from dipping deep at the card table, in my opinion, is far more likely to be the reason for her attacking my sister and then leaving here like a thief in the night.'

'My lady, as I said, my view is controversial. The study of the human brain, the emotions that make up one's personality, is in its infancy. Many doctors still believe that harsh treatment, beating, starvation and confinement are the best treatments for any mental disorder.'

'Mama isn't mad, she's somewhat eccentric, extremely selfish and very spoilt.' Amanda stared at the doctor almost daring him to contradict.

'I'm sure that she is all those things, Lady Amanda, but I still think it might be worth my while talking to her myself. Sometimes conversation with a thoughtful stranger can be very beneficial in these circumstances. I believe that his grace wishes me to do what I can to smooth things over.'

Miss Westley, who wasn't given to interrupting, spoke out for the first time. 'Doctor Peterson, I am governess to Lady Elizabeth. His grace has given me permission to speak to you about her disabilities in the hope that you might be able to help me prepare her for her future.'

'I should be delighted to meet Lady Elizabeth.' He turned to Amanda and nodded politely. 'Do I have your permission to do so, my lady?'

For a moment Sarah thought her sister would refuse but then she nodded. 'Yes, thank you, that would be most kind of you. Richard said you were an expert in matters of the mind. Do you also treat more common ailments too?'

'Are you referring to Lady Sarah's ankle? I should be happy to examine it and see if she's ready to abandon her crutch and walk unaided.'

Everyone was now standing. 'I'll return to my apartment shortly, sir, and will wait there for you. You must see our sister first as that is far more important.'

'I don't expect our mother to be back today. Would it be possible for you to return in a few days and talk to her?'

8

Paul didn't envy the duke his confrontation with his future mother-in-law. It was bound to be acrimonious and the outcome unpleasant — certainly for her grace.

'We've been up all night, gentlemen, I suggest that we get a few hours' shut-eye. Our quarry will be doing the same and, much as I wish to get this matter settled and return home for my nuptials, she's an elderly lady and I've no wish to make her unwell by insisting she makes the return journey before she's had time to rest.'

The mention of sleep made Paul yawn and soon all three of them were doing so. 'What time do you wish us to be on duty again, your grace?'

'It's not quite six o'clock. I think we should reconvene at noon. Thank you for accompanying me on this adventure. I own I enjoyed the ride despite the reason for it. I'm finding that civilian life can be somewhat tame after being a soldier for so long.'

The duke strode off lost in thought leaving Robinson and himself to follow. 'It's just occurred to me that the duke's stallion is easily recognisable. I wonder if one of the grooms will send a message to her grace?'

'There's nothing much we can do about it, sir. As his grace said, the carriage is going nowhere with one of the team lame.'

Paul shrugged. 'In which case, we'll do as suggested and get our heads down for a few hours.'

Sharing a chamber with his ensign after having had the luxury of single occupancy was a reminder that when he became an active soldier, with only his pay to live on, he was unlikely to have accommodation of any sort.

Most regiments provided officers with a tent and a cot to sleep in but everything else had to be provided from one's own pocket. He had initially been delighted to get the opportunity to buy a captaincy in the duke's old regiment but now he wasn't so sure.

They'd both removed their boots, stocks and topcoats but nothing else. Not only was he sharing the room he also had to share a bed. Despite the fact that it was wide enough for several sleepers he found it difficult to settle especially as Robinson was asleep the moment his head hit the pillow. Until now he'd no idea his junior officer snored quite so loudly.

He'd been told by more experienced officers that when on campaign one had to snatch sleep whenever one could. He must learn that skill but, despite the fact that he'd been up all night and ridden across country for hours, it eluded him.

For some reason every time he was drifting off his head was filled with images of Sarah. She was way above his touch and he must put his burgeoning feelings for her firmly to one side. A duke's daughter would marry someone from her class. Even if she was interested her guardian would refuse his permission.

Eventually he slept but was woken by someone hammering on the door what seemed like scarcely half an hour later. He might find it difficult to fall asleep but was always instantly awake, alert and fully functioning. Robinson was still snoring and he shoved him off the bed.

In two steps he was at the door and had it open. He'd expected to find his grace waiting to speak to him but it was the landlord.

'There's a frightful ruckus started in my snug. I reckon the sight of two soldiers will soon put a stop to it.'

'We are provost marshals, not regular army. Our concern is for the behaviour of common soldiers, not civilians.'

'That's what I said — it's a recruiting officer that's causing all the trouble.'

Robinson was now on his feet and clumping about behind him.

'Two minutes, and we will be down.'

He checked his pistol was loaded but prayed he wouldn't have to use it. After strapping on his sword, he pulled it from in its scabbard a couple of times to ensure it would come out smoothly if required.

Both he and Robinson were back in their scarlet coats, their stocks tied, and were ready to descend and put a stop to the nonsense he could hear as soon as he stepped from the door.

'Do we arrest him?'

'If we do, we'll then have to find somewhere to take him. I don't know how far the nearest barracks is from here.'

'I didn't know they had recruiting officers wandering about in the wilds of Lincolnshire, sir. I know there's a barracks at Colchester but I doubt the man will be based there.'

'Good point, Robinson. I believe that there might be one in Norwich which is no great distance from here. I wonder if this so-called recruiting officer is a charlatan. Although I can't see how he hopes to gain financially as it's he that has to give money and buy beverages to those he recruits, rather than the other way around.'

The sound of shouting and breaking furniture coming from the front of the building made him increase his pace and he took the last stairs at the double. He drew his pistol and burst into the chaos of fighting, drunken men.

★ ★ ★

Sarah had written the letter to the vicar but decided to take it in person and at the same time take two footmen with as many garden blooms as they could carry. 'Amanda, I misremember if there are suitable receptacles for flowers anywhere in the family chapel — do you know?'

'I believe there are some in the small alcove on the left of the door. It's fortuitous that the chapel is a separate building and a sufficient distance from the demolition of our ancestral home to be usable for my wedding tomorrow.'

'I must wait here until the doctor has examined my ankle but will leave immediately after that. I take it you are on your way upstairs to be with Beth whilst he talks to her.'

'I am. I'm tardy and must hurry. I like the man, but he does have revolutionary ideas about treating people with mental instability.'

'I'm going to speak to the head gardener although am loathe to do so as he is one of the many who has worked for the family for thirty years or more. If Richard does decide to dismiss them, then we will be woefully short of staff.'

'I'm certain he won't send anyone away who makes it plain that they're loyal to the family name rather than just to our mother.'

'I've been wondering if it's possible those involved didn't know they were being disloyal. After all, they'd spent their lifetimes following mama's orders to the letter so why should they think they could refuse to do so now?'

'Sarah, dearest, the fact that they were asked to take her away in the middle of the night would be reason enough to suspect there was something going on that shouldn't be. I do understand your point that they might not have felt themselves in a position to refuse outright — but any one of them, if loyal to Richard, could have alerted him.'

'Which reminds me, how did he discover she'd gone?'

'He was obliged to get up and for some reason decided to check the door remained locked. He discovered the room empty and the rest you know.'

'Also, I can't believe that no one else in the household was unaware of the trunks being removed or that no one in the accommodation used by the grooms was aware that the carriage and seven horses had been put to.'

'Which brings us full circle, does it not? The only reason for the resounding silence was because either they were too frightened to speak up or because they approved of what was taking place. Not a happy thought. I've always considered we had a good atmosphere here and that the staff were well-treated. Therefore, it's a mystery to me why they should betray

149

us in this way.'

Sarah hopped across and hugged her. 'Put it from your mind, my love, and think about tomorrow when you will become the Duchess of Denchester.'

They parted company, she to make her slow and clumsy way outside to find the head gardener and her sister to go to the attic and participate in the informal consultation taking place on the nursery floor. She could hardly go in search of the man. She beckoned one of the young footmen to her side.

'I wish to speak to Jimmy, the head gardener, immediately. I'll be in the study. I don't expect to be kept waiting.'

'I'll fetch him at once, my lady. He'll not tarry, I give you my word.' The young man was sturdily built and if she remembered rightly the gardener was a small man of middle years and she rather thought he'd be unwise to argue with the person sent to fetch him.

She scarcely had time to sit behind the desk when she was alerted to hurrying footsteps. She smiled at the thought that one pair must belong to the footman but the others were someone in his stockinged feet. Jimmy had been obliged to remove his boots before answering his summons.

The door was open and the gardener was all but bundled through it. He bowed. 'Beggin' your pardon, my lady, it ain't right for me to be in here not in me dirt but this young varmint made me come.'

'At my insistence, Jimmy.' She smiled her thanks at the messenger and he bowed and moved out of view, but she was certain he was standing to attention beside the door in case he was needed. This was one member of staff they had no need to question about his loyalty.

'Lady Amanda is to be married tomorrow evening and I want all the flowers you can find in the garden and the hothouses brought in. There must be enough to decorate the family chapel and the entrance hall and dining room.'

She was half-expecting a surly response but instead his eyes lit up and he smiled broadly. 'Married tomorrow? Now that's the best news I've heard all year. I ain't one of those what helped last night. Me and my lads never knew nothing about it until we was up.'

'I'm glad to hear it. If you had woken, what would you have done?'

'I'd have rung the fire bell, my lady, that would have stopped them.' He paused and half-closed his eyes as if lost in thought and then nodded to himself. 'It ain't right what happened. I reckon his grace ain't too pleased neither. There's only a handful what turned a blind eye.'

'I'm relieved that you've told me. Could I prevail upon you to tell me the names of those you mentioned? His grace will not wish to dismiss the wrong members of staff.'

He was only too eager to assist and soon she had the necessary names to give Richard when he returned. There were only seven which was gratifying as at one point both she and Amanda had thought that more than half the staff might be disloyal and have to be dismissed.

She didn't bother to get up to ring the bell but merely raised her voice slightly. 'Would you be kind enough to escort Jimmy from the premises and then ask the housekeeper to attend me here?'

The footman appeared as if by magic. 'Right away, my lady.'

'Before you go, I need to know your name. You must be new as I think I'm aware of all the others employed here.'

'Tom Black, my lady, at your service. I started two months ago.'

'Then welcome to the household, Tom. I'm certain you will do well here.'

★ ★ ★

Paul erupted into the snug and without hesitation fired his weapon into the air. The noise, in so confined a space, was deafening and the reek of cordite enough to make one choke. It had the desired effect and the men fell apart as if pulled by invisible strings.

'What the devil's going on here? Where is the recruiting officer who has caused this fuss?'

The man who stood up was wearing a recognisable uniform, but it had seen better days. In fact, on closer inspection it was the only item of clothing the man had on that was of a military origin.

The culprit staggered to his feet and made a sloppy attempt at a salute. 'Corporal Jenkins reporting for duty, sir.'

'Arrest that man, Mr Robinson, and march him outside and then confine him in a suitable shed.' Times must be desperate indeed if the half a dozen, crawler infested, specimens in here were anything to go by.

'Are you serious about joining the military?'

'We is, your honour. It ain't that far to Norwich. If that bugger won't take us then we'll find our way ourselves.'

'I suggest that before you set out you do the best you can to improve your appearance.' He dipped into his pocket and handed the man, who appeared to be the spokesperson for the group, a handful of coins. 'This should be enough to get yourself a square meal and help pay for your passage. Good luck with your endeavours.'

The landlord stepped in and was about to snatch the money from the man's hand but Paul intervened. 'Prepare a bill for the breakages and present it to me. These men are going to fight for King and Country and will need the little I've given them to get themselves to Norwich.'

He thought the landlord was going to protest but suddenly his demeanour changed. Paul glanced round and saw the duke had joined them.

'What's going on? I was woken by the racket and came to investigate.'

Paul quickly explained and the duke nodded. 'I approve of your actions but there's no need for you to be out of pocket. You wouldn't have been involved if I hadn't asked you to accompany me.' He snapped his fingers and held out his hand and the man dropped the coins in.

'Here, I'll take care of this. Do you know what you're going to do with the so-called recruiting officer?'

'No idea. I'm going to wait for him to sober up and then hopefully he can tell us what he was doing here and why these men believed him to be something he obviously isn't.'

He wasn't sure if he was offended by having his money returned or grateful that his benefactor had stepped in. He smiled. A handful of coppers and silver coins was a mere bagatelle to the duke but the man understood that he and Robinson were not in so fortunate a position.

Robinson was outside talking to the would-be recruiting officer who was leaning somewhat haphazardly against the wall. Paul was about to join them when he became aware that he was being observed by a group of men who looked vaguely familiar.

He strode across, using his height and military bearing to establish his superiority. These were the grooms and outriders who had shown such disloyalty to their employer.

'His grace is temporally engaged elsewhere but will be out to speak with you men about your reprehensible behaviour. After you have been dismissed without reference you will see the error of your ways.'

They shuffled from foot to foot and refused to meet his eye. Then a wiry individual with bald pate and shifty eyes spoke up.

'All of us here have been working for her grace all our adult lives. The old duke being dead we naturally transferred our allegiance to her grace.'

'His grace employs you and pays your wages not the Dowager Duchess.' He looked from one to the other and settled his gaze on the one he believed to be the coachman. 'You, step forward.'

Reluctantly the man moved towards him. 'Yes, sir, how can I be of service?'

'Why did you continue when your lead horse was lame?'

'Her grace was determined to reach The Coach and Horses and weren't prepared to walk.'

'If his grace was aware that one of your outrider's mounts went under harness as well as saddle then you must have known this too. You're a disgrace to your profession.'

The duke spoke from behind him. 'Well said, Captain Marchand.'

There could be no doubt that the duke was an officer to his core. He fixed the trembling group with an arctic glare before speaking again.

'I believe that Captain Marchand has already informed you that I no longer require your services.' He dipped into his pocket and tossed a golden guinea to the coachman. 'There's sufficient here for your journey back. You'll collect your belongings and any remuneration you might be owed and then depart without reference.' He turned his back on them and spoke to him.

'Mr Marchand, have you had the opportunity to examine the lame horse?'

'I have not, your grace, but will gladly do so if you would be kind enough to excuse me for a few minutes whilst I speak to the corporal who caused the disturbance earlier.'

'I'll accompany you, I'm curious to know why that disreputable old man was mistaken for a recruiting officer.'

The story when told was less interesting than the event it had preceded. The ex-soldier had made no claim to be anyone but himself and it had been the scurrilous group who had made this erroneous assumption.

Paul was pleased the duke once more handed over a few coins and the matter was closed. 'I'll check on the condition of the injured animal, your grace, and ensure that the others are recovering from their labours.'

'Good man. I'm intending to return first thing tomorrow. I want to be back in time to get married in the afternoon.'

Now all his grace had to do was persuade the indomitable old lady upstairs to agree to return. He didn't envy the duke that task. He'd rather face the French than the Dowager Duchess.

9

Richard hoped that he hadn't picked up any unwanted visitors from the unwashed men he'd been in contact with. The inn was a smart establishment and he was somewhat bemused by the fact the landlord had allowed these men to drink in his snug.

He was on his way to speak to the errant dowager but decided to find an answer to this puzzle before he did so. He was procrastinating — dreading the confrontation. He wasn't close to his future mother-in-law but for the girls' sake he was determined to keep his personal feelings to one side.

He headed back to the tap room where the fracas had taken place. He noticed immediately something he'd missed before — this section of the building was separated from the main part by solid doors. The snug was now deserted and the broken stools and table had been removed. The door at the far end stood open letting in welcome fresh air.

He glanced upwards and smiled when he saw a bullet hole in the ceiling. No doubt that would be a talking point in future amongst the locals. This explained how the less sanitary locals were able to access this place but why the landlord needed their business he'd no idea.

'Your grace, is there something I can help you with?' The landlord himself came in through the door.

'Two things I'm curious about. First — it's scarcely morning and yet this room was filled with drunken men. How did that come about? Secondly — why would a prestigious coaching inn such as this allow that sort of person entry here?'

'I came from such ordinary stock, your grace, and was fortunate to marry the daughter of the owner of this place. Those men were once respectable and laboured on the local farm but were laid off a few months back and have found no further employment. I've been allowing them to sleep here occasionally.' He smiled ruefully. 'Jed, a distant cousin of mine, found two shillings on the cobbles and invited his friends in to drink it away. I'd like to thank you for your generosity in helping them out.'

'Thank you for your explanation. Has her grace sent for refreshments or hot water?'

The man beamed. 'Both were taken up half an hour ago, your grace.'

Richard could delay no longer. If he wanted to be married to his beloved girl tomorrow evening as planned then he had no choice but to get this confrontation over with.

He paused outside the door to marshal his thoughts. It belatedly occurred to him that there was no apparent reason for her sudden departure. After all, had he not already agreed that she could move to the estate in Northumbria as soon as he'd ensured the place was habitable?

Was he missing something here or was this just another example of her disturbed state of mind?

His knock was somewhat louder than

162

he'd intended but had the desired result. The door was opened immediately. The maid clutched the door frame. Her colour faded.

'Your grace, it's his grace,' she managed to whisper before stepping back to allow him to enter.

He stepped into a spacious sitting room and was relieved it wasn't the bedchamber. The duchess remained seated. Her lips thinned and her eyes narrowed. Unlike her servant, his unexpected appearance hadn't shocked her.

He nodded and crossed the floor to stand towering above her. This wasn't the time for pleasantries or reconciliation. If he wanted to persuade her to return, without being obliged to carry her kicking and screaming to her carriage, he must be firm. He must make a case so strong that to refuse to obey would make no sense even to her.

'Madam, your behaviour is unacceptable. Those that accompanied you have lost their positions and will leave without references because of it.'

She blinked but remained silent. He continued, keeping his tone glacial and his expression hard.

'Not only that, but your insistence on continuing when one of my team was lame has unnecessarily ruined a good horse.'

Again, she refused to answer. He rarely lost his temper but her intransigence, his lack of sleep and the disruption to his wedding pushed him too far.

'God dammit to hell! What's wrong with you? Are you so lost in your own conceit and selfishness that you act with no consideration for others at all? Why the devil run off like that when all you had to do was wait another sennight and you could have left with my blessing and support?'

This finally elicited a response. 'How dare you use such language in my presence? It would have been better if you had remained in Corunna and met your end there. I'm certain there must be someone better to fill the position you hold so poorly.'

Her answer was so extraordinary that he couldn't keep back his snort of laughter. This enraged her further and she surged to her feet. She was obviously expecting him to step backwards. He braced himself and she collided with him. He gripped her elbows and prevented her from striking him.

'That will do, madam. Control yourself. You do yourself no favours by behaving like a demented fishwife.'

She was practically gibbering with rage. The more she stuttered and abused him the funnier he found it. He knew he was exacerbating the situation but he couldn't help himself.

He lifted her from her feet and put her back on the settle. 'Stay where you are. I apologise for laughing but I can assure you my amusement is better than my fury.'

The two maids had vanished into the adjoining room and firmly closed the door behind them. Hardly the actions of loyal servants who should have remained at her side to support her.

Then to his horror her tirade was replaced by sobs. It was impossible to remain angry with a woman in tears. He pulled out his handkerchief and sat beside her.

'Take this, my dear, I apologise for upsetting you. I hate to be at daggers drawn and don't understand why we've come to this pass when I thought we were good friends.'

She took his offering but continued to shiver and cry. He put his arm around her shoulders and drew her to him. For a moment she resisted but then relaxed against him and he rubbed her back and murmured words of comfort until she regained control.

Between sniffs and gulps she blew her nose and mopped her eyes. He'd expected her to stiffen, to move away from him, but she remained within his embrace.

'Richard, I don't know what's happening to me. One minute I'm calm and happy the next in a fearful rage and I've no idea why.'

'This is not because I stopped you gambling?'

Now she pulled away and looked at him as if he was the one with a mental imbalance. 'My gambling? Why would you say that? Have I not kept my word?'

'Recall the scene in the drawing room, my dear. When I reprimanded you for trying to bully the young officers into dipping deep you knocked over the card table and . . . '

Her eyes widened. 'I don't remember that. How dreadful — what must you have thought of me?'

Richard was now seriously concerned. He'd been blaming her for her behaviour when it appeared she was seriously unwell.

'I hate to upset you further, but you also attacked Sarah before taking off in the middle of the night in my carriage.'

Tears trickled down her ashen cheeks. 'I don't remember that either. I do recall waking up and being convinced that I must leave for Northumbria at once.' She gripped his hand painfully. 'What's happening to me, Richard? Am I afflicted with the same disease that our poor dear King is suffering from?'

'I don't know, but I promise you we'll find out. Whatever happens, I'll not send you away. Your girls and I will take care of you.'

'Please, don't dismiss those that helped me.'

'I've already done so. However, I'll provide them with references and sufficient funds to tide them over until they find other employment. I'm afraid that's the best I can do.'

She nodded and managed a weak smile. 'Thank you, you're a dear boy, and whatever I might have said to the contrary, please ignore it.' Her face was ravaged by grief and he wished it hadn't come to this before the true extent of her illness had been discovered.

'Amanda and I intend to get married tomorrow in a small family ceremony. That means we must set out at dawn tomorrow in order to be home in time. Will you be recovered by then?'

'I don't know how I'll be by then. Promise me that you will make me return whatever I might say or do. I appear to have no control over my behaviour and no recollection of the episodes of rage that you describe.'

'I was wondering if I can have permission to address you as Mama? You will hold that position very soon.'

'I don't deserve your kindness, I cannot believe there's another gentleman in the world who would treat me so kindly after what I've done.'

He placed a light kiss on the top of her head and was about to leave her to the ministrations of her maids when she grabbed his hand a second time.

'You must incarcerate me in an asylum if I become violent, Richard, I cannot bear the thought that I might hurt one of those that I love so dearly.'

'I give you my word that whatever the outcome of this illness you will remain with us. If at times you are . . . you are disturbed then you'll be confined to your apartment until the episode passes.'

He left her, saddened by what had taken place. He knew little about the workings of the human brain but he had seen men behave irrationally after having received a serious head injury. Was it possible she had struck her head at some time unknown to any of them?

★ ★ ★

Sarah took her sister's place and slipped in quietly to the nursery where Beth was so entranced by what Dr Peterson was saying to her that she didn't even look up. Miss Westley seemed equally mesmerised by what was taking place.

'Lady Elizabeth, what is your favourite occupation?'

'I know, I know the answer to that. I like to play with my dolls and my very favourite is this.' Her sister held up the one she was holding in her arms. 'She's called Arabella — don't you think that a pretty name?'

'I do indeed, my lady. If you could not have a doll to play with what might you do instead?'

'I like to draw, to go into the garden or to have someone read to me. I don't often like horses or dogs but I do like cats. Can I have a cat for myself, Miss Westley?'

'That's something you must ask his grace when he returns.'

Beth pouted. 'Why has he gone away and where is my mama? I don't like it when things are different. I don't like this nursery either I like the one at the other house.'

Sarah was going to intervene as she could see a tantrum coming on but the doctor raised his hand slightly indicating that he wished to see how things developed.

'I believe that the duke has gone on a trip with your mama but will be back tomorrow.' He gestured around the nursery. 'I think this a delightful room. Why don't you like it?'

'It's not the other nursery. I want to go back there. I want to go back there right now.' She scrambled up from the floor where she'd been sitting cross-legged and hurled her favourite doll across the room. The delicate porcelain head smashed when it hit the wall.

Beth threw herself on the floor and began to scream and drum her feet on the carpet. This hadn't happened for a year or more as always someone intervened with a distraction before her sister became wild with fury and quite uncontrollable.

Both she and Miss Westley were on their feet about to drop down and try and reason with the screaming girl.

'No, my lady, Miss Westley, let it play out. In my experience it's best for a child to release their anger as long as there is no danger of hurting themselves or others. The time to talk is afterwards when they're calm.'

'Are you quite sure, sir, that to be so enraged is good for her with her delicate mental constitution?'

'Yes, quite sure, my lady. What would have happened if you had lost your temper in this way at her age?'

Without hesitation Sarah answered. 'I only did it once and was soundly spanked for doing so. I never made that mistake again.'

'Then perhaps you should do the same for your sister. She won't learn to control her emotions if you give in to her every demand.'

'Beth is not a child in her body but only in her mind. It would be quite wrong to physically chastise her.'

'My lady, if you wish your sister to be able to participate in family occasions she must learn to behave appropriately. Imagine the scandal it would cause if she did this when you had guests.'

Miss Westley had been listening closely. 'I think the doctor has made a good point, my lady. I agree that Beth should not be smacked but she must be disciplined for her behaviour. Although her favourite doll is now broken, which is a severe punishment in itself, I shall make her sit with her face to the wall for an hour until she learns that this sort of performance is not acceptable.'

The racket coming from the floor had abated. Her sister sat up, her face blotched with tears and her nose running, waiting to be embraced and comforted as always happened.

'Beth, I'm most displeased with you. Your behaviour is quite disgraceful and you can consider yourself fortunate that Richard is not here as he might well have administered a sound spanking which you so richly deserve.' Sarah surprised herself by the severity of her tone.

'I need a kiss. I'm very sad now because my doll is broken.' Beth had deliberately ignored the threat but Sarah knew she'd registered what had been said.

Miss Westley stood, unsmiling, beside Beth. 'You will get up immediately, young lady. Take that chair to the corner and sit on it facing the wall. You will remain there until I give you leave to move.'

The doctor had moved away but Sarah was aware he was listening carefully.

'I'm very sorry I've been a naughty girl. Can I have some cake now?'

'You cannot. Get up immediately and

174

do as you're told.' Sarah hated to be so firm and prayed this might be the one and only time it would be necessary.

Beth looked from her to Miss Westley and saw no support from her governess. She got to her feet, picked up the chair and carried it to the far corner of the nursery and then sat on it facing the wall as she'd been bid without another word.

Sarah's heart was pounding. She hated confrontation and unpleasantness of any sort. She blinked away unwanted tears and followed Miss Westley and the doctor into the passageway where they could converse without being overheard by the miscreant.

'That was well done indeed, ladies, I think it highly unlikely there will be another performance like that. Lady Elizabeth is obviously severely limited in what she can achieve but I've heard of six-year-olds writing a concerto, being able to paint a beautiful picture — I see no reason why she shouldn't have a fulfilling life.'

'There's something that really worries me, sir, and that is the fact that she might have the emotional feelings of an adult but not the intelligence to deal with them. Could she fall in love with a gentleman and wish to . . . wish to take things further?'

'I think you're correct to be worried about that eventuality, my lady. Therefore, I suggest you don't let her attend public events where she could come in contact with such a person. Being an heiress could make her a target for an unscrupulous fortune hunter.'

'Oh dear! That's exactly what we feared. She loves to dance and to wear pretty gowns but has already had one unfortunate experience where she was mistaken for myself when we were at Vauxhall Gardens.'

'I believe that Lady Amanda is to marry his grace tomorrow evening. No doubt there will be an addition to the family sometime next year. If Lady Elizabeth was to be allowed to play a substantial part in looking after any niece or nephew, that might well be enough to keep her contented.'

Miss Westley moved so she could see if Beth had remained on the chair. 'She's sitting there as instructed. Tell me, sir, are we to offer comfort and treats when she's completed her punishment or will she still be in disgrace?'

'I think a middle road would be the most beneficial in this situation. What would you normally do at that time of day?'

'We would complete whatever lessons had been started at nine o'clock and then nursery luncheon would be served up here. After that we go outside if it's fine and study the flora and fauna in the grounds. The specimens we collect will then be drawn the next day.'

'I should move about the schoolroom as if nothing untoward is taking place. If she attempts to stand up insist she takes her place again. When you consider her punishment is done quietly tell her to sit at her desk and resume her studies.'

Miss Westley smiled. 'Thank you so much for your assistance. I can see now that we've indulged her when we should have been firmer. What about the doll?'

'If it's possible to have it mended, then do so. If not then just remove it without comment.'

'Doctor Peterson, this has been most informative. Perhaps you could look at my ankle as I've spent too long up here already.'

There was a window seat at the far end of the wide passageway and she took her place. Miss Westley remained quietly at her side to ensure that no protocol had been breached. His touch was gentle and he rewound the bandage before speaking to her.

'I suggest that you continue to use your crutch until you can put your foot down without pain. However, if you inadvertently put weight on it there won't be any permanent damage. It's healing well.'

She smiled her thanks and left Miss Westley with the doctor. Neither of them seemed in a hurry to end the visit. Their lively chatter followed her on her slow progress to the door.

10

Paul checked on the horses and discovered that the injury to the carriage horse wasn't as bad as he'd feared. The farrier had removed the shoe from the offending hoof, filed it down and replaced it with a new one.

'That'll do, sir, sound as a bell now. If you ain't going nowhere until tomorrow you'll have no problems.'

'That's good news.' The duke had given him sufficient funds to pay and the man went away happy with the transaction. He was aware that those who'd been summarily dismissed were slouched in a corner looking far from happy. They'd all worked for the Sinclair family for decades and must feel they'd had a raw deal as they'd only been doing their duty as they saw it.

An impulse made him walk across to speak to them. He handed each one of them a crown and immediately their demeanour improved. 'This should be sufficient for you to pay for a seat on the next stage and give you a little left over until you find yourselves another position.'

They suddenly straightened and for a second he thought it was because of his offer but then his grace spoke from beside him. 'I've changed my mind. Her grace has asked me to reinstate you and I've decided to indulge her.' The men were now exchanging happy smiles. The duke hadn't finished. 'Your loyalty is to me, not to any other member of my household. If you forget that a second time then I'll not be so lenient. Do I make myself quite clear?'

There was a chorus of assent and all of them nodded, bowed and touched their foreheads demonstrating their respect and delight in his generosity.

'Your grace, all four carriage horses will be fit to make the return journey tomorrow morning.'

He was slapped vigorously on the back. 'Excellent news. Walk with me — we need to talk.'

Paul was curious as to why this could be so but fell in beside him without argument.

'I take it things are smoothed over with her grace.'

'They are indeed. This is between us and in the strictest confidence. We both fear she has the same affliction as the King. Her bursts of vicious temper happen without her knowledge and she appears to have no control over them. It's a very sad case and one that deserves sympathy rather than condemnation.'

'I'm sorry to hear that, your grace. I assume that you will take care of her at home and not have her incarcerated in an asylum.'

'Exactly so. I hope that quack will be able to shed some light on this affliction. I'm hoping we might be given pointers to the warning signs of an attack and can then can confine her safely until she's recovered.'

'Forgive me for asking, sir, but is there a history of insanity in the family?'

He laughed out loud startling two

grooms who were busy harnessing two horses to a waiting carriage. 'I hope you're not suggesting I'm showing signs of being unbalanced myself? As far as I know this is the first case.'

'As we're private, your grace, there's something I most particularly wish to discuss with you. I'm no longer certain that I wish to remain in the army. Unfortunately, I can't think of anything else that I might do to support myself.'

'You have no prospects, I take it?'

'None at all. My father, Sir Robert Marchand, inherited a large estate and sufficient funds to live comfortably. However, he also inherited my grandfather's addiction to gambling. Need I say more?'

'That explains why you were able to refuse her grace when she tried to force you into playing for high stakes. So, are you the eldest son? Do you inherit the title and the debts? Do you have siblings or a mother still alive?'

'I'm an only child, which in the circumstances is fortuitous. My mother, whom

I love dearly, is living with her sister and acting as an unpaid and undervalued companion.'

'Not with your father?'

'God knows where he is — he abandoned the family home several years ago. When I inherit the title, I'll inherit nothing else but, as you so rightly pointed out, a mortgaged estate and a pile of debts.'

'I can see why you used what little you had to purchase your colours. I need to get this business with Patrick resolved and need your help to do that. If you still wish to sell out then I'm in need of an estate manager — I've recently dismissed mine for malfeasance. Do you have any experience in this field?'

'I do indeed, your grace. Before my father bankrupted us, I was in charge of our demesne. I took over on reaching my majority and was turning a tidy profit before he lost everything.'

'You scarcely look old enough to have reached your majority now — how old are you?'

He smiled. 'I'm four and twenty, your

grace. I was fortunate that I remained an ensign for only a few months before being able to purchase this captaincy. My mama has a small annuity and had been saving it for years in order to help me establish myself. It's because of her lack of funds that she was obliged to take up this demeaning position with her sister.'

'Do you think she would be prepared to take on the responsibility of both carer and companion to my future mother-in-law? I can assure you she would be well remunerated and treated with the utmost respect.'

Paul was overwhelmed by this offer. The duke scarcely knew him and yet was prepared to go out of his way to help him and his beloved mother.

'I'm certain she would be delighted to take up your kind offer. I too would be honoured to be your estate manager. I shall resign as soon as Mr O'Riley's no longer in danger of being arrested and sent to fight.'

It soon became apparent that he knew

184

more about running a large estate than the duke. His companion appeared unbothered by this lack of knowledge on his part.

'I've been a soldier all my life and had no expectations of having an estate to manage. Men — military matters — even financial things — I'm an expert with those. I worked as quartermaster for a year or two so know how to organise and balance the books.'

'I grew up thinking I would be inheriting a substantial demesne and spent much of my formative years following the estate manager around and learning as much as I could. I was too young to understand that my father was gambling everything away.'

* * *

Richard couldn't believe his luck. Patrick could fulfil his role as his man of affairs admirably but knew as little about estate management as he.

'I assume that you only became an

officer as you had no alternative.'

'That's correct, your grace. It didn't occur to me to apply for a position as an estate manager for which I'd be better suited.'

'If you had, then it would have been my loss. I have an escritoire in my apartment. Come with me and you can write at once to your mother and tell her the good news. Where is she residing at present?'

'In Hertfordshire, your grace. I think I'll write to Horse Guards and tender my resignation at the same time. I'll state the reason for my sudden decision as my dismal failure to capture the deserter.'

'I'll send my carriage to collect Lady Marchand. I have a second team that will go as well as the horses that are here.'

'I would like your permission to go with it and explain in person what will be expected of Mama when she arrives. I should have made it clear that she's little more than forty years of age and looks younger. She was married at the tender age of sixteen.'

'I worked that out for myself, March-and. Let's repair to my apartment as I wish to write to Amanda. I can then frank the letters and get them sent by express.'

He dashed off a short note to Amanda.

My dearest Amanda
I shall be returning with your mother tomorrow and everything has been resolved. I am looking forward to our wedding.
Richard

He read it through, sanded it, and was about to fold the paper neatly and seal it by pressing his ducal ring into the molten wax.

'God's teeth, Marchand, what can you possibly be writing that's taking you so long?'

The young man looked up and grinned. 'Are you telling me, your grace, that you have already finished your *billet-doux*?'

'I'm not given to romantical flourishes. A letter is for conveying information — nothing more.'

'Lady Amanda is about to become your wife, your grace . . .'

'And that's another thing, I'm damned sick of being referred to so formally. Call me Sinclair if you must or Richard if you will. I'll call you Paul.'

'I was saying, Richard, that you should be telling your bride-to-be how much you love her, how much you miss her, give her something to put under her pillow and dream about.'

'Would you care to read it?'

'Good God — I should think not. I'm only suggesting that you do more than just convey facts.'

'I suppose it's rather brief and to the point and certainly not in any way a love letter. As you still have your resignation to pen I'll start again.'

My dearest love
You will be relieved to know that I'll be returning tomorrow with your mother. Things have been rectified and I'll give you the details on my return. She is unwell not deliberately behaving badly.

He stared at the paper unable to think of what he might write to the girl he loved more than life itself. The girl without whom he would be bereft. Now he understood what Paul was trying to tell him. It was all very well thinking such things but he needed to grit his teeth and put them down on paper.

I'm sorry to have left you with the arrangements for our wedding. I love you, darling girl, and cannot wait to tie the knot.
Richard

His companion looked up with a smile. 'I take it you've been more successful this time. I have finished the correspondence for my mother and will be done with the letter to Horse Guards in a few moments.'

When all three missives were sealed and ready to be dispatched something occurred to him. 'What about your ensign, Robinson? Do you think he will continue in his career or also wish to resign?'

'I think he'll wish to stay. Why not send him with the letters to your former commanding officer instead of me?'

'I shall do that. I'll also ensure that he has sufficient funds not only to become a lieutenant but also to buy a captaincy when one might become available and he has the experience to assume a position of command.'

'I'm at a loss to understand why you should have taken it upon yourself to help both of us in this way.'

'I've more money than I, or my family, can spend in a lifetime. Why not to use it to benefit others less fortunate?'

'A laudable sentiment, your . . . Richard. If all those with wealth and influence shared your beliefs then there'd been no unrest amongst the workingmen. Shall I take the letters downstairs for you?'

'Yes, do that. This is a post office and I'm certain there'll be a mail coach leaving here every hour or two. They can go by express and will be there tonight.'

He returned to spend an hour with the duchess, who he now referred to as

Mama, she was looking a little better than she had earlier.

'I think an intimate wedding service and private celebration will be perfect, my dear boy. Do you think that my girls will be able to arrange it at such short notice?'

'I'm sure of it. There's something else I'd like to tell you.' He then regaled her with his plans for Paul and Robinson and for some reason she seemed less enthusiastic than he'd expected.

'You do realise what will happen if we throw Sarah and this young man together?'

'I'm employing him to run my estate, he'll hardly be a member of the family.'

For the first time that day she laughed and the sound pleased him although the reason for it did not.

'I can assure you that the two of them will want to make a match of it. Will you give your consent to your ward marrying a commoner?'

★ ★ ★

Sarah spoke to the vicar and he was, naturally, only too happy to accommodate his benefactor in any way he could.

'I shall be ready to conduct the service whenever his grace and Lady Amanda wish me to. I shall have my wife and daughters arrange these lovely flowers immediately, Lady Sarah.'

'That would be most helpful, Mr Carstairs. As you can see, I'm somewhat incommoded by this ankle. I believe there is some restriction as to the hour when a wedding can take place, is there not?'

'That's for a special licence, my lady. As the banns have been correctly read and the ceremony is to take place in a consecrated building then I can see no difficulty whatever the time might be. I understand that travelling can be hazardous even in the summer.'

'We are expecting them home late afternoon but it's a relief to know things can still go ahead even if they are delayed somewhat.'

On her return she discovered that Dr

Peterson had now departed with a promise to return the following day.

'He could have left it longer, Amanda, I don't think his services will be required on your wedding day.'

'It wasn't I that suggested he return so soon but Miss Westley. He had departed before I could contradict her suggestion. What did you think of him — as a physician?'

'His suggestions for managing Beth made absolute sense. He's a personable gentleman and a considerable improvement on the old-fashioned and curmudgeonly doctor who is the only medical man in this neighbourhood.'

'It's a long ride from Ipswich which is hardly satisfactory in an emergency. I did like him and thought him intelligent and knowledgeable. Perhaps Richard will be able to persuade him to move nearer with the promise of being our personal physician.'

'If he's also to attend to everyone employed by the family, those in the cottages and farms then it might well be worth his while.' Sarah caught a flash of white in the garden and walked across to the window. 'I see that Beth's now released from her chair and is taking her usual afternoon constitutional. I noticed that Miss Westley was paying particular attention to everything the doctor said — do you think that has any other significance?'

Amanda laughed. 'Good heavens, they've only just become acquainted. I hardly think they will have developed an interest in each other so soon.'

Sarah thought it best not to contradict this by telling her it had only taken half an hour for her to wish to further her association with Captain Marchand. One might have thought her interest had been caused by his smart red uniform but in truth she preferred him wearing civilian clothes even if they were those of her deceased papa.

She was confident that her curiosity about this handsome gentleman remained undetected because Richard would never agree to a liaison with a penniless commoner, especially as he was about to depart to fight and could possibly be gone for years.

They dined simply and Miss Westley joined them. 'I must apologise for inviting Doctor Peterson back without first eliciting your consent, Lady Amanda. I thought you would wish her grace to be examined immediately she returned.'

'As we are unaware exactly when they will be here, it might be better to postpone his visit until the following day. I take it you now have his address?'

'Good gracious me! I do not. How silly of me not to have asked.'

Sarah immediately reassured her. 'Richard's the only one who knows as he was the one who sent for him. However, I'm surprised he agreed when he knows there is to be a family wedding tomorrow evening.'

MissWestleycoloured.'Iconvincedhim that beginning his treatment of her grace was paramount. Again, I overstepped my boundaries and I most sincerely apologise.'

'Fiddlesticks to that! Richard and I will be delighted to have another guest attend our nuptials.'

'Do you intend to take a wedding trip, Amanda? And what about your bride clothes? I believe it's customary to replace one's wardrobe before marrying.'

'I've more than enough gowns to last me a lifetime. Whilst it would be a pleasure to spend a few weeks away with Richard in the circumstances that cannot happen. No doubt we'll have other opportunities to travel when things have been resolved here.'

'If I ever marry . . . '

'What a thing to say, Sarah dearest. Of course you'll be married and sooner rather than later I suspect. As long as you marry a local gentleman, I'll ensure that Richard gives his permission whoever it might be.'

'As far as I recall from the party we held last Christmas, Amanda, my choice is severely limited. Those that are eligible are either too old or too stupid to be of any interest to me. I intend to remain here and be a devoted aunt to your children.'

This remark was greeted with the laughter she intended. They decided to sit on the terrace as the evening was warm and it was far too early to retire. Scarcely an hour later the butler appeared with a letter that had arrived by express. He held out the silver salver and Amanda removed the square of paper.

11

Paul had anticipated that his ensign would be disgusted at his abandoning the army so casually. The reverse was true.

'That's splendid news, sir. Permit me to say that I think you will make a better estate manager than you will an officer.'

'Why do you say that? I thought I had all the necessary requirements to do my job efficiently.'

'I've always wanted to buy my colours, to fight for King and Country, but this was an expedient choice for you. To be successful I believe you must have a burning desire to be an officer and not be there by default.' Robinson smiled. 'You're an excellent officer, but your heart isn't in it.'

This was the longest speech his ensign had ever made and it somewhat surprised him. 'Thank you for being so plain-speaking. I must own that I felt as if a weight had lifted from my shoulders when I signed my letter of resignation and handed it over to be delivered to Horse Guards.'

'This does not, I fear, solve the problem of the missing sergeant major. Am I now to take the letters to his grace's former commander in Portugal?'

'Indeed you are. His grace intends to help you in your career in return for your service. I can see him coming with the missives in his hand.'

Paul half-bowed as did Robinson and this gesture was returned with a slight inclination of the head. 'Excellent. Mr Robinson, I take it you're aware of the change in circumstances?'

The young man nodded. 'I am, your grace, and eager to get on my way and have this matter settled fairly for your man.'

The duke handed over the papers and a large purse of coins. 'There's gold here to pay your way. One of the letters is a recommendation that you be taken on as a lieutenant in my old company. The other explains the circumstances.'

Paul was sorry to say goodbye to his companion but delighted for the reason of their parting.

The following morning he was reluctant to don his uniform but had nothing else to wear. He was up at dawn and hurried down to inspect the carriage team. The lead horse that had been lame was now fully recovered and they would be able to depart as soon as the duchess and her companion came down.

The return journey was conducted at a more decorous pace than their arrival. He and the duke rode ahead of the carriage to avoid the dust it kicked up. They halted twice for an hour to allow the horses to rest and the passengers to alight and stretch their legs.

On the second break he was called to the side of her grace. 'Young man, I understand that you've resigned your commission and will now work for his grace.'

He bowed. 'That is correct, ma'am.'

'You will inherit a title on your father's

demise, but nothing else?'

His employer had obviously been discussing his background. 'A minor baronetcy, your grace, and as far as I know my father is presently in good health.'

He was puzzled as to why he was getting this interrogation. He must suppose her grace believed it her business to grill anyone who was employed by the duke.

'I do not expect you to spend time with my daughter, Sarah, she is above your touch.'

Paul couldn't prevent his snort of laughter. He tried to hide it with a cough but was unsuccessful. He waited for a massive set down but to his astonishment she smiled.

'Excellent, I knew you to be an intelligent and sensible young man. I like you well enough but you understand how things are.'

'I do, your grace. I give you my word as a gentleman that I shall treat Lady Sarah with the utmost respect and at no time overstep my place.'

The conversation was over and he

nodded politely and wandered back to join the duke who was checking the girth of his stallion. 'What was that all about?'

'I was told in no uncertain terms that Lady Sarah is out of bounds. I cannot imagine why her grace believed I thought myself a suitable candidate for her daughter's hand.'

'I apologise if her comments caused offence. She has a bee in her bonnet about the two of you forming an attachment just because you'll be living under the same roof.'

'I can assure you, sir, I'm not pursuing Lady Sarah. I'm in no position to make any young lady an offer and getting leg-shackled is something that's in the distant future.'

'Then I have nothing to worry about on that score. You will be less conspicuous once dressed in civilian attire.'

'I have none of that, your grace, until I can see a tailor.'

'Continue to wear my predecessor's garments until that can be achieved.' The duke gestured to the ladies that they clamber back into the vehicle.

Once mounted he spoke again. 'I intend to gallop ahead. I wish to reassure my bride that I'm actually going to be present for our ceremony. I rely on you to take care of things in my absence.'

He cantered off and Paul reined back and allowed the carriage to go past him. As he was to be in charge for the remainder of the journey he would have a better view from the rear.

He began to recognise landmarks and thought they were probably no more than twenty miles from their destination. He turned in the saddle on hearing the sound of a horse approaching. The rider was easily identified from his size. This was the missing sergeant major. Why was O'Riley putting himself in danger of being arrested?

★　★　★

Sarah was now able to walk without using her crutch although she did have a slight limp. She was overseeing the flower arrangements in the dining room in preparation for the evening celebration when her sister came in.

'This looks quite delightful, dearest, I just hope that Richard arrives in time for the ceremony to take place.'

'As Mama and he are reconciled and she's quite willing to return I'm certain they'll make good time. I'm going to ride over to the church and make sure the flowers are equally pretty there. Do you wish to come with me?'

'That's exactly what I would like. I can't remember the last time you wished to ride out. Are you quite sure your injured ankle is up to the experience?'

'It will be the other one that's in the stirrup so I'm certain I'll have no difficulty.'

'What has persuaded you to resume this pastime?'

'Beth was talking about being scared of horses and I decided that if she saw me riding she might be prepared to try again after her scare.'

'Have you already sent word to the

stables or shall I do that?'

'I haven't — which is fortuitous as I didn't know you were intending to accompany me. I'll be perfectly happy with Star as she's gentle and quiet. Your stallion, Othello, and she are the best of friends so there would be no difficulty between them. Which mount are you taking instead?'

'There are several suitable horses in the stable and any one of htem willsuffice.'

Half an hour later they were walking sedately down the drive accompanied by a footman on a handsome bay gelding who kept a respectful distance to the rear.

'I find it hard to credit that tomorrow I'll be a duchess and married to Richard. To think that I didn't even know he existed until he turned up in January this year.'

'When I decide to tie the knot, I'm now determined it will be to a gentleman from this neighbourhood. I've no wish to move so far away that I cannot visit as often as I wish to.'

'Mama invited suitable candidates to my nuptials and Richard intended to cancel those invitations. This would have caused unnecessary unpleasantness if they'd been the only ones who'd had their invite retracted.'

'Then it's a good thing your original plans to hold a ball have been put aside. It would be pleasant indeed to have, perhaps, a garden party later in the summer and invite our neighbours and those that are employed by the estate.'

Her sister wasn't listening but peering over the hedge at something the other side. 'Poor little things — where did you come from?'

Sarah guided her docile mare to the edge of the path and looked over at what had upset Amanda. Three half-starved puppies whined and attempted to scramble through the branches.

'Benson, you must collect those three unfortunate animals and take them back. Make sure that they are fed first and then bathed and found a comfortable corner in a stable.'

The groom stood in his stirrups, peered over the hedge, and grinned. 'I'll not be able to carry more than two, my lady. I'll go and get a sack . . . '

'You'll do no such thing. They must be wrapped safely in something and carried under your arm. Bring another groom to assist you.'

The puppies were too weak to push their way through the thick foliage and the sound of their pitiful yapping was heart-rending as they thought they were being abandoned.

'Who could do such a cruel thing? I wonder where the mother is? Do you think they're old enough to be away from her?'

'It's hard to tell as they're so emaciated. I think it likely that the mother went in search of food and was injured and unable to return for them. I fear there might have been more than three in the litter and the others have perished already.'

Sarah came to a decision. 'I'm sure

the flowers are perfectly arranged, so we must take a puppy each. They might well be infested with fleas but I cannot bear to leave them another moment.'

Fortunately, Benson was still with them. 'You stop there, my ladies, I'll get the little varmints and hand them up to you. If you wrap them in a fold of your habit the crawlers won't get no further.'

There was a gate a hundred yards along the lane and they went through and trotted their mounts down the field until they reached the animals.

Their groom handed her a smelly, bedraggled female and she wrapped it lovingly in her skirt. It was impossible to tell the colour of the puppy's coat beneath the dirt. Amanda took another and Benson tucked the third into a commodious pocket.

'Are there any more puppies in the hedge?' Sarah asked anxiously.

'No, my lady, nor dead ones neither. I reckon these little mites wouldn't have survived another day if we hadn't found them.'

They returned at a canter and she prayed they were in time. Their sudden arrival caused consternation in the stable yard.

Amanda quickly explained and the puppies were taken away to be fed. She held out her sadly mired skirt. 'I fear this will need more than a quick sponge to rectify the damage. We must go in at once and have these laundered before the unwelcome visitors escape elsewhere.'

Beth must have seen them return and was waiting in the hall, her eyes wide. 'Why are you back? Did something happen?' She made a move to approach but Sarah shook her head.

'No, darling, don't come close as I fear we have unwelcome visitors on our habits.' When she told her sister the reason she was delighted.

'Can I go and see them? Can we have them in the house? Will one of them be mine as there are three puppies?' She was dancing from foot to foot. 'I like puppies now not cats.'

Miss Westley smiled at her charge.

'Allow your sisters to change, Lady Beth. I'm certain that they will wish to see how the new arrivals are progressing when they are freshly garbed.'

'But can I keep one for myself?'

Amanda was already halfway up the stairs but called back. 'We shall see, sweetheart. It depends if Richard is open to the idea of having canines in the family. I know that our mama dislikes them which is why we've never had an indoor pet.'

'Is Mama coming home today? I don't like it when she's not here.'

'She will be back in time for Amanda's wedding, Beth. Now shouldn't you be attending to your schoolwork? Remember, if you wish to attend an evening event you must be a good girl all day.'

Their soiled garments were placed in a laundry sack and taken away to be dealt with by a chambermaid. Freshly gowned she and her sister were ready to descend.

'I noticed that your personal items and clothing have already been transferred to the master suite. It will be strange to be in this apartment on my own as we've shared our accommodation for so long.'

Amanda hugged her. 'Fiddlesticks to that! I'm moving to the other end of the corridor not the other end of the country.'

Sarah returned her embrace but her eyes were damp. From tomorrow Amanda's time would be filled with marital duties of one sort or another and she would have little time for anything else.

* * *

Richard's arrival was anticipated and two grooms were waiting to take his horse, leaving him to travel at the double to the side entrance that was the nearest to the stables.

He'd heard a church clock strike four times and prayed that he wasn't so late the ceremony couldn't take place today. He refused to go another night without making love to his darling girl and would anticipate his wedding vows if necessary.

'Richard, I didn't expect you so soon.'

She flung herself into his arms and made it quite clear that she was as eager as he to consummate the union. Her cheeks were flushed delightfully when she stepped away. 'I'm just about to go up and change. Your bathwater will be on its way to your chamber as we speak.'

'My love, I've so much to tell you. But I'm in no state to continue our conversation so it will have to wait until I'm less malodorous.'

'I love you in whatever state you're in. It's fortunate indeed that I haven't already changed into my wedding finery.'

Hand in hand they ran up the staircase. He pulled her close for a second time as they reached his apartment. 'This is the last time you'll have to go elsewhere to change.' Belatedly he remembered he had not asked about the well-being of his other charges. 'Is everything and everyone in my household as it should be?'

'You've only been gone a short while, darling, so of course we're all perfectly well. Sarah's ankle has recovered enough for her to walk without assistance. Beth is overexcited about the wedding. Doctor Peterson has given us some useful information about handling her and will return soon to examine Mama.' She paused and then continued. 'And we now have three rescued puppies as part of the household.'

'Dogs? I love them but not in the house unless they are vermin free and house-trained.'

'They are none of those things at present. So, we can keep them?'

'You can have whatever you want, sweetheart. I refuse to remain here conversing in my dirt. The carriage is about an hour behind. There'll be ample opportunity to exchange news whilst we wait for the others to arrive. I doubt that we'll get to the chapel before seven o'clock. Will that be breaking any ecumenical rules?'

'Mr Carstairs assured me that as the banns have already been called there's no restriction on the hour as far as he's concerned. I think that there might be some regulation stipulating we cannot be married after five o'clock but I don't think anyone would have the temerity to question the legality of our union, do you?'

'I don't give a damn. As long as we've exchanged our vows and have a certificate to prove it then that's good enough for me.'

Somehow he managed to refrain from kissing her again and allowed her to dash off to get ready. He was surprised that neither Sarah nor Beth had come to greet him, but perhaps they were unaware of his having arrived so soon.

★ ★ ★

He'd half-expected her to be waiting in his sitting room — soon to be their sitting room — but it was empty when he strode out freshly garbed and more fragrant than he had been previously.

There was ample time for him to inspect the floral arrangements in the dining room, speak to the butler and ensure that baths would be waiting for

214

the others when they arrived.

Amanda joined him on the terrace looking even more beautiful in a gown of pink silk which emphasised her curves and set off her glorious hair to perfection. He stepped forward intending to kiss her but she shook her head and smiled.

'No, I wish to remain tidy. Look,' she said and pointed to the drive, 'the carriage is approaching and will be here soon. Good heavens — where is the other officer?'

He quickly explained and she looked less than delighted by his news.

'Mr Marchand cannot reside with us, Richard, unless you wish him to form an attachment to my sister and for Sarah to become betrothed before the end of the summer. I think he should make his home at the Dower House. I'm sure a soldier won't object to a little dust and noise.'

'Your mother will approve of that arrangement as she too is worried and considers that having them in constant company isn't a good idea. However, I spoke to Marchand and he assured me that he has no intention of setting up his nursery any time soon. He has nothing to offer and needs to make his way in the world first.'

'My sister has now decided that she's eager to find herself a husband as long he is from this vicinity. Mr Marchand will eventually be Sir Paul Marchand and with her fortune at his disposal he might come to consider himself a suitable candidate.'

He was about to tell her that Marchand was the last person he would want as a brother-in-law, but then said something else entirely. 'He's an excellent young man and I wouldn't stand in their way if they wished to make a match of it. They could have this house when ours is finished.'

'Then we are in accord, my love, as I, despite what I said earlier, also believe he might be the right gentleman for her. If he's living elsewhere then there will be time for them to decide if they'll suit. I presume as your estate manager that he'll be in a similar position to Miss Westley? Neither one thing nor the other.'

'As far as I'm concerned I consider him on equal footing to myself. No — don't raise your eyebrows at me, Amanda. Until six months ago I was merely an officer in his Majesty's army and was more a reluctant duke than one eager to take up my responsibilities.'

'Richard, I'm sure that Mr O'Riley is accompanying the carriage and riding beside Mr Marchand. Why has he returned? Won't he be arrested when that unpleasant soldier returns from London?'

'Don't fret, sweetheart, everything's in hand. I sent a letter by express to catch Patrick on the road and ask him to return. I think it highly unlikely there'll be further nonsense from Horse Guards after my intervention.'

12

Paul had enjoyed the remainder of the journey getting to know his unexpected companion and they were now on first name terms. 'Patrick, her grace should have ample time to prepare for the ceremony.'

'That she will, my friend. I'm glad that I've now got the opportunity to witness the wedding. I just hope the duke's confidence isn't unfounded and I'm in no danger of being arrested and forced to sign up for another five years.'

'As I'm no longer part of the military, I'm quite prepared to lie for you. Unless they bring someone from your former regiment to identify you there's no actual proof that you are the person the general's seeking.'

'I scarcely recognise myself with brown hair and grand clothes. I doubt that there's anyone in England who knows me personally, apart from his grace.

Even if there was, no comrade of mine would speak up and have me arrested.'

Their arrival was expected and a bevy of footmen were waiting to collect the luggage. The two grooms who'd accompanied her grace on her aborted journey were ready to take the reins of his horse and that of Patrick.

He stood by the door of the carriage and offered his arm to the dowager but she waved him away.

'Thank you, young man, but I'm perfectly capable of disembarking from a carriage without assistance.'

He stepped aside ready to assist if needed. She might be mentally impaired but she was a sprightly lady and descended as if she was a lady half her age. His mama would be a perfect match for her. Her three daughters rushed from the house to greet her and it warmed his heart to see them embrace so lovingly despite what had taken place before.

Should he go in the front door as he had done previously or would he now use the staff entrance at the side of the house? His employer appeared in the doorway.

'Marchand, don't dither about there, come in, there are things I need to discuss with you before we set out for the chapel.'

Patrick had followed the ladies through the front door. He was obviously comfortable with his position in the household.

He followed his employer to the study and was there informed that the next day he was to move to the Dower House and set up his office there. This suited him as he had no wish to intrude on the family.

'Patrick will be joining you there. No doubt you'll need to appoint a clerk or two to assist you with your work. I've already sent sufficient staff over to get things ready for you both.'

'I can move in tonight . . . '

'There's no need. Stay and celebrate with me. I'm taking my bride away for a short trip which will give you time to familiarise yourself with what's required of you in your new position.'

The meeting continued for so long that he scarcely had a quarter of an hour to remove his uniform for the last time, complete his ablutions and change into one of the borrowed outfits so he could attend the wedding. The duke had left in a gig with Patrick, the ladies — including the bride — had taken the carriage that had just returned, but with a fresh team in the harness.

There was a handsome gelding waiting for him outside the front door. All eventualities had been prepared for and he was impressed. Being on horseback meant that he soon caught up with the carriages. The wedding party was small and he was privileged to be part of it.

The small chapel was full of garden flowers and the aroma of these almost masked the smell of damp that one always found in a building of this antiquity.

They remained standing, even the dowager, and the reverend gentleman began to conduct the ceremony. There were no hymns, no homily, and no prayers. Therefore, in less than half an hour it was done and the new duchess, looking radiant, walked out on the arm of her husband.

Her mother followed with the younger daughter and her companion, which left him to walk beside Sarah.

'That was brief but poignant and I'm honoured to have been included.' He smiled down at her and was surprised at the warmth of her response.

'Richard has explained that you're now part of the household and will be running his estates for him. It will be most enjoyable having both you and Mr O'Riley joining us for dinner most evenings.'

'We will both be living at the Dower House.' She looked somewhat dismayed by his answer so he quickly changed the subject. 'I'm glad to see that you're scarcely limping, my lady. Your ankle has healed well.'

'Richard has assured me there will be dancing after we have dined as Miss Westley has agreed to play for us. Are you as proficient as he on the dance floor?'

'As I've not had the privilege of watching his grace perform it would be difficult to compare our abilities, my lady.' He had reverted to formality when addressing her as his position was now different.

Her eyes sparkled. She appreciated his teasing response.

'From your evasive answer I must deduce that you can dance — it remains to be seen whether I consider you a match for Richard.' Her smile rocked him on his feet. 'Did you know that there's to be a garden party which will include an informal dance on an evening next month?'

'I wasn't aware of that information, thank you for telling me. No doubt his grace will require both Mr O'Riley and myself to organise this event.'

She grasped his arm impulsively. 'Oh, Mr Marchand, do say that you will allow me to help you with the planning?' She too had abandoned the use of his given name.

Gently he moved his arm so her hand

fell away. 'If his grace gives his permission then I should be delighted to have your assistance, my lady.'

They walked in side by side chattering as if he was an old friend and not someone who was little more than an acquaintance. Thank God he was moving from this house tomorrow as spending time with this lovely girl would be a disaster for both of them.

* * *

Sarah walked beside him, her pulse racing. Was she more excited about getting to know Paul or the fact that she was going to be involved in planning the garden party? That Richard would give his permission she had no doubt, he was bound to be in a benevolent mood now he was married to her sister.

They parted company as soon as they stepped in and she rather thought he wasn't sure of his place in the hierarchy and had no wish to possibly offend by escorting her. She was saddened that he believed he must remain formal from now on.

Her lips curved as she recalled what had transpired just before the family had departed for the chapel. Her forget-me-not blue gown and matching accessories had been made especially for today and she was confident that she looked her best.

Her maid had told her so before she'd gone downstairs. 'That's the perfect colour for you, my lady, it exactly matches your eyes. Do you require the parasol or will the bonnet be sufficient?'

'No parasol, thank you.' After smoothing the blue kid gloves over her wrists, she had picked up her skirts and hurried to the door. There had been no necessity to take a reticule as they would only be gone an hour or so at the most.

Beth had emerged from the nursery floor bouncing from foot to foot. 'You look so pretty, Sarah. I love that gown. Do you like mine?' Her sister had twirled showing her silk stockings and the pretty pink slippers made especially to go with her new ensemble.

'It's quite delightful. Don't do that or you'll dislodge your bonnet. I believe I can hear our mama downstairs so we must hurry.'

They had then left for the chapel in the hastily cleaned travelling carriage.

★ ★ ★

Her sister had behaved impeccably and one would never have known from mama's behaviour that she wasn't perfectly well. To think that Amanda was now the Duchess of Denchester, that their mother was no longer in charge of the household — not that Mama had actually done anything much as it had all been left to Amanda to do since Papa had died.

The small party was assembling in the dining room which was overflowing with sweet smelling flowers perfect for their small celebration. It was now past eight o'clock and much later than they usually dined.

The finest napery, silverware and crystal had been set out around the table and the eight of them took their places. Richard and Amanda were, of course, at the head. Beth, Miss Westley and Mr O'Riley took seats to the left of them and she, Mama and Paul arranged themselves on the right.

Richard remained on his feet obviously intending to make a speech of some sort. Champagne was served and even Beth was given a small quantity. She had accepted a glass but didn't intend to sip more than a mouthful.

'I shall keep this brief. I just want to say that this is the happiest day of my life. How I persuaded this wonderful girl to marry me, I've no idea. I would like to thank my new mama, Sarah and Beth for making me welcome and a part of their family.' He paused, raised his glass and turned to look at her sister who was incandescent with happiness. 'To my bride and to our future together.'

They raised their glasses and drank to the happy couple. Although Amanda had asked for a simple meal Cook had disregarded her wishes and there were several courses each with half a dozen removes. Obviously, the kitchen wished to make it plain that they were as delighted about the nuptials as were the family.

The conversation was lively, the champagne flowed and by the time her sister stood two hours had gone by and it was long past Beth's bedtime. Richard refused to remain behind to drink port with the other two gentlemen and followed his wife into the drawing room.

'Sarah, I know we agreed there should be a waltz or two but I'm not sure in the circumstances it would be wise.'

There was no need for her sister to say that they were all far too full to skip about and a great deal of champagne had been consumed — goodness knows how much more the gentlemen had imbibed than the ladies.

'Beth has retired with Miss Westley, Mama is hiding her yawns behind her hand, so I think I'll be content with a stroll in the garden.'

Mr O'Riley bowed and bid everyone good night which just left the four of them. Richard had his arm around Amanda's waist and was whispering into her ear. Sarah didn't know exactly what took place in the marital bed but wasn't so naïve that she didn't understand the newly married couple were eager to retire.

'Mr Marchand, would you be kind enough to accompany me to the lake and back? Good night Richard, good night Amanda. Your wedding was perfect and the wedding breakfast quite delicious.'

Only as she was about to make her way down the granite steps to the formal gardens did she realise that she shouldn't be wandering about in the dark on her own with a gentleman. Fortunately, for both of their reputations, he was more awake to the dangers than she.

'Forgive me, Lady Sarah, but I think it too late to walk about the grounds. I should be delighted to accompany you tomorrow but I too am fatigued after the long journey.'

'I'd quite forgotten about your mad dash through the countryside to find my mother. I apologise — what was I thinking?'

She spun, curtsied and without bidding him a good night, fled back into the house alone. He was a most unsettling sort of gentleman and she regretted her impulsive request to work with him on the planning of the summer party.

Her maid was waiting to help her disrobe and soon her lovely gown was safely in the closet. As she slipped into bed everything was different and it wasn't just the fact that her sister was no longer in the adjacent bedchamber. Something else had changed. Was it her mother's mental instability that was causing her to feel so agitated or was it something else entirely?

* * *

Richard had his arm lightly around Amanda's waist as he guided her through the house and towards his now to be shared accommodation. She was trembling beneath his touch. Instead of going directly into his bedchamber he took her to the sitting room.

'My darling, there's nothing to be afraid of. What happens between a man and his wife is a joyful experience for both of them. I give you my word that I'll do nothing to upset you.'

She stepped away from him but kept his hand in hers. 'It's not fear but excitement which makes me shake. I love you so much and wish to learn everything there is to know about being a wife.'

He snatched her up in his arms and barged through the communicating door. His valet and her dresser had been told to wait until they were called for before putting in an appearance.

She sat where he placed her on the edge of the vast tester bed and watched him rip off his clothes with unfeigned interest. He cursed his clumsiness and hopped from foot to foot in an effort to remove his boots.

Her laugh filled the chamber. 'Let me

help you, my love, and then you can help me.'

In record time they tumbled, as nature intended, into bed.

Some hours later he propped himself on his elbow to watch her sleep. If the good Lord chose to take him this very moment, he could die a happy man. He'd had his share of amorous relationships but nothing had prepared him for this. Sharing his body with the woman he loved was more than he could have dreamt of.

He understood now why men and women did such foolish things in the name of love. He was a changed man. From this moment forward he would love her, keep her safe, do everything in his power to make her as happy as he was.

Her glorious hair was spread across the pillows and tenderly he removed the strands that were resting across her face. Her eyes flickered open.

'Good morning, husband. Is it time to get up already?'

He leaned down and kissed her. 'Absolutely not.'

When eventually hunger drove them from between the sheets the sun was already beginning to set. He pulled on his bedrobe and she did the same.

She tilted her head and sniffed. 'I can smell rose water — I believe our wishes have been anticipated and there might be a bath awaiting us.'

He moved across to the newfangled bathing room that his predecessor had installed here and pushed the door open with his foot. The waft of fragrant steam confirmed her suspicions.

'You bathe first, sweetheart, I'll organise for some trays to be fetched.' He looked around his chamber. Garments were strewn across the floor and the less said about the bed the better. 'We shall decamp to your room, darling, and leave the maids to put this straight.'

She drifted past him but paused to stand on tiptoes and place a loving kiss his lips. 'I never thought to marry and especially not someone as handsome and wonderful as you. I don't understand how you can call me beautiful when I have such a disfigurement.'

He drew her close. 'I told you when I first saw the scars caused by your riding accident some years ago that they would be no barrier to finding love. You scarcely limp at all nowadays, it's only perceptible when you're tired or upset. I don't give a damn about it and never have. I love you inside and out and that will never change.'

Before he could make good on his intentions she was gone and he heard her stepping into the bath. He poured cold water into the basin and plunged his head in. It had the required effect and he was now no longer embarrassed by his desire and could safely pull the bell-strap.

He was tempted to join her but decided against it. When she emerged, her cheeks flushed and her eyes sparkling, it took all his self-control to keep her at arm's length.

'There's a cold collation set out in the sitting room. To accompany our repast there's freshly made lemonade, champagne and coffee — I wasn't sure which you would prefer.'

'Coffee is exactly what I want. Forgive me, but I'm so hungry I intend to start without you.'

'There's more than enough there for several meals. I won't be long.' As he was luxuriating in the tepid water he remembered that he'd neglected to tell her they were to go away the following morning.

He sat up so abruptly a deluge slopped over the side. He ignored it. 'Sweetheart,' he yelled, 'tomorrow I'm taking you to the coast for a week. I have a small estate overlooking the sea . . . '

The door flew open and she stood, a sandwich clutched in one hand, and stared at him. 'There's no need to shout in that unmannerly fashion, Richard. You're no longer on the parade ground.'

He grinned. 'I beg your pardon, my love. Is that for me?'

'It certainly isn't. If you wish to eat then you must get out of that bath. Eating in the bath? What an extraordinary suggestion!'

The appetising aroma of horseradish and beef from her hand curtailed his ablutions. He stood up sending a second tidal wave onto the boards. His years as a military man, having little time for personal care, meant he was dried and beside her in minutes.

'Here you are, dearest, I've prepared this for you.' She handed him a plate piled with bread and meat. 'There's coffee on the table. I've never been to the beach — thank you so much for arranging a wedding trip even if it is only to be for a sennight.'

'I thought we could take the barouche rather than a closed carriage. What do you think?'

'I suppose we'll have to take your valet and my maid as well as luggage and two grooms.'

She sounded so despondent at the prospect that he chuckled. 'It's no more than three hours and would be less if we rode. Would you prefer to do that? Then our servants can travel in the carriage with our bags.'

'There's a phaeton in the coach house — what I'd really like to do is have you drive me in that.'

He considered her request for a moment and then nodded. 'Then that's what we'll do. If we get up at first light we can be there in time for breakfast. I've already sent half a dozen staff ahead of us to prepare the house.'

'I'm impressed by your efficiency, my dear. When did you have time to organise this?'

'I'm a military man to my core, darling girl, not an effete aristocrat. Become accustomed to my ability to set things in motion when necessary.'

She curtsied and her bedrobe parted. He discarded his food and held out his hand. She came to him willingly. Some considerable time later they returned to the buffet and the food tasted none the worse for the wait.

13

Paul settled into his new abode with Patrick and was satisfied his life had taken a turn for the better. They had a cook, several maids, a footman, plus a groom to take care of the horses. There were already outside men employed for the upkeep of the extensive grounds of the Denchester family estate whilst the new edifice was built.

A pony cart was employed to bring all the necessary ledgers and documents from Radley Manor so both himself and Patrick could take care of their duties efficiently. Overall control remained with the duke and Paul sincerely hoped that he'd not removed items that were no concern of his.

Patrick reassured him. 'He'll not bite your head off if you have. He's right fierce if you cross him but's always a fair man. Didn't hold with flogging, and discipline in his brigade was the better for it.'

'I need to go to Ipswich and find myself a tailor. I don't intend to continue wearing the garments of a dead duke any longer than I have to. I can't see that there's anything pressing for me to do today — I've set up interviews with the factor for tomorrow morning and will then begin to visit all the properties in the locality.'

'I've papers to take to the lawyers' office in Ipswich so we can ride together. It's no more than an hour and a half from here so we'll get there and back easily before dark.'

Paul was fortunate to have had recommended to him a tailor who had a small shop away from the main street. He made his selections, was measured, paid a substantial deposit to show he was in good faith, and was told the first of his jackets, waistcoats and breeches would be ready the following week.

The stooped old man handed him a brown paper wrapped parcel. 'There you are, sir, three shirts, a dozen stocks and half a dozen pairs of stockings. I thank you for your custom and will have the first outfit delivered to you as soon as maybe.'

'Excellent. I have an hour or so to spare so is there somewhere particular you would recommend that I go to admire?'

'It's always busy at the port and well worth a look. I bid you good day, Mr Marchand.'

Using the directions given to him Paul walked briskly in the direction of the river. The town was busy, the noise of manufacturing echoed from several streets. The pedestrians appeared well-dressed and looked prosperous. Mind you he avoided the poorer areas — it would be unwise for someone like himself to wander there unescorted.

He'd agreed to meet up with Patrick at a local hostelry to dine at six o'clock. This gave him ample time to explore the town that would be the centre of his life from now on. He passed an assembly room and saw that there was to be a subscription ball to be held that very evening.

The port had a dozen or more ships tied up along the riverbank and he spent a happy hour watching as cargoes were loaded and unloaded. Reluctantly he turned and made his way to the agreed meeting place.

Patrick had yet to arrive so he ordered a tankard of porter and found himself a quiet corner to wait. By seven o'clock he was seriously concerned about the absence of his friend. He tossed a few coins to the barman and headed for the street in which the lawyers' office was situated.

He bounded up the steps and marched into the vestibule. The clerk all but fell from his stool at his precipitate arrival.

'My friend, Mr O'Riley, his grace, the Duke of Denchester's man of business, was here earlier. What time did he leave?'

'Mr O'Riley departed two hours ago, sir.'

'Did he say where he was going?'

'Not to me, sir, but I'll ask Mr Culley to speak to you if you would be kind enough to wait.'

The clerk returned and this time he was accompanied by a younger man — presumably Mr Culley.

'Mr O'Riley said he was going to the port and then to meet a friend at The Kings Head. I assume, sir, you are the gentleman he was referring to.'

'I am. I waited over an hour but he failed to appear. I was at the port myself earlier but didn't see him. He's head and shoulders above most men and I'm sure if he'd been there I would have seen him.'

'This is most disturbing news. To whom do I have the honour of speaking?'

'I am Marchand, recently appointed as estate manager to his grace.' Paul offered his hand and the lawyer shook it. He decided to take a chance and explain why the disappearance of O'Riley was such a concern.

'There's something you need to know. We need to converse in private.'

He was ushered to a large, well-appointed office which had two windows overlooking a pretty garden. This man must be a senior partner to have such a chamber. He quickly explained the circumstances.

'Then I have the worst possible news for you. My clerk has reported seeing four redcoats loitering on the other side of the street several times this week. I fear Mr O'Riley has been apprehended.'

'God's teeth! We should have taken you into our confidence at the start and then you could have warned him. His grace has taken his new duchess for a short wedding trip to a small estate that overlooks the sea near Norwich. I'm hoping that you might have his destination.'

'I certainly do, I know exactly where his grace has gone.'

Once he had the name and directions, he left the premises at a run. His instructions were clear and he knew the landmarks he was to look out for if he travelled across country. He collected his mount and left sufficient blunt to pay for the keep of Patrick's horse until it could be collected.

Both he and his gelding were blown when they thundered to the front door of the manor house, scattering gravel as he pulled the beast into a rearing halt. It was now almost dark and his arrival had not been seen from the house.

He pulled the reins over the animal's ears and hoped it would remain where it was until a groom could attend to its needs. His thunderous knocking was answered immediately.

He stepped around the shocked footman. 'I need to speak to his grace urgently.'

'His grace has retired. More than my life's worth to disturb him, sir.'

'Then tell me which chamber he's in and I'll rouse him myself. This matter cannot wait.'

★ ★ ★

Richard, having just made passionate love to his wife, was relaxing, satiated and content when someone had the temerity to hammer on the door. Before he could react a voice he recognised spoke loudly to him.

'Your grace, forgive me for disturbing you, but Patrick has been taken. Four soldiers were waiting outside the lawyers' office and he has been gone since five o'clock.'

Amanda was sitting up beside him, the bedsheet clutched under her chin, her eyes wide. 'You must go, my love. His safety is paramount. I'll return home tomorrow and await you there.'

He kissed her but his mind was already focusing on this disaster. He was dressed and ready to ride scarcely a quarter of an hour after being roused. He discovered Paul devouring a meat sandwich in the entrance hall, an empty tankard beside him.

'My horse is done. I've taken the liberty of having two of your carriage horses saddled. They are both up to our weight but unfamiliar with being ridden which might well make our journey interesting.'

'Good man. The only way they could

have taken Patrick was if they knocked him insensible. This will make it hard for them to transport him and, when he does come around, he will make things as difficult as possible in the hope that we'll catch up with him.

'Riding pell-mell at dead of night is becoming a habit with us, Paul. I have a list of possible places they might have put up for the night. Patrick will no doubt be incarcerated in a suitable out-house which should make it easier for us to release him.'

The two massive carriage horses were cavorting and rearing and it took two grooms to hold the head of his whilst he mounted. No sooner had they released their grip than he was subjected to a series of massive bucks. There was no time to take note of what was happening to his companion — the man was an expert horseman and would do as well as he.

His teeth were jangling in his head by the time he mastered the horse, but he was still aboard and fortunately, so was his companion. 'Paul, I'll follow as you can use the route you arrived by.'

This time there was a full moon which made their headlong gallop less dangerous. Wisely the man in front avoided massive hedges and ditches when possible as neither animal would have much experience of jumping having spent their working life pulling a heavy carriage.

A distant church clock struck one when he saw they were approaching a small town. When both horses were walking he was able to speak to his companion.

'Is this the first of the places you think Patrick might be?'

'It is, your grace . . . ' The young man was obviously no longer comfortable addressing him as Richard as he was now his employer.

'Cut rope, Paul. I cannot abide being addressed so formally by someone I now consider a friend. If you can't bring yourself to call me Richard any more, then I'll answer to major instead.'

'Thank you, major. I'm comfortable with that. Mr Culley supplied me with four possible venues and this is the first of them. We both decided it was unlikely they would attempt to take him anywhere he might be recognised as your man of business. Therefore, all the addresses I've been given are for smaller inns off the main route to Colchester.'

'If we check the stables that will tell us immediately if Patrick's hidden here.'

He dismounted in a small meadow behind the inn they were going to investigate. The horses were tethered to the fence and seemed content to remain there whilst they recovered. Fortunately, there were no other occupants as this might have caused a problem.

This time he was in front and he walked soft-footed towards the rear of the outbuildings. The snuffling of other horses could be heard but, so far, no vigilant canines had set up a racket. He found the back gate and it was unlocked.

It was unlikely that any small establishment would have five similar horses in their stalls at the one time. Also, military tack would be easily recognised.

Their search was fruitless and they were mounted and were on their way to the next place in minutes. He was confident their visit would remain clandestine.

They repeated the process at two more places without success. The next, the furthest from Ipswich, was their last hope of finding Patrick and effecting a rescue. Paul raised his hand indicating they should halt.

He leaned across and whispered. 'There are five horses in the field behind this inn, major. I believe we've found him.'

'Then we must be vigilant. A good commander would mount a guard however unlikely he thought a rescue might be.'

'I'm unarmed. Do you have a weapon?'

'Two loaded pistols.' From the light of the moon it was easy to hand one over, as well as the powder and shot. Satisfied the young man was competent he loaded his own and dropped it into his coat pocket.

The horses had travelled fast but would

be able to continue after a short rest. They were cool as the distance between the four establishments had been short.

'There's a trough by the gate, Paul, let them drink before we begin our search. In fact, I think it might be wise to catch one of the others and get a bridle on it so we can make a quick exit.'

Voices carried in the night and they continued to converse in whispers. They were lucky that the paddock with the horses was some distance from the buildings allowing them to do what was needed without being overheard.

'The largest horse will suit. He can ride bareback as easily as on a saddle, which makes things easier. There are halters hanging from the gate — one of those will do at a pinch.'

The gelding was happy to leave the others and they tethered him alongside their own mounts before going in search of their missing friend.

★ ★ ★

Sarah was up and dressed early as she was eager to see how the puppies were doing. Reports from the stables had so far been encouraging but she wished to see for herself this morning if they were going to survive their unfortunate start in life.

The house was pristine, the floors still damp from being recently scrubbed, and there was already a footman on duty to open the side door for her. The noise coming from the stable yard indicated that the grooms were taking care of the numerous horses that were owned by the family. There wasn't room for all of them to be inside but she was sure they enjoyed the freedom of a field in this clement weather.

Her arrival had been observed and the head groom was waiting to greet her. He touched his cap and bowed. 'Good morning, my lady. You come to see the little pups? You'll not recognise them from the bedraggled specimens brought in two days ago.'

'They have recovered well?'

'They have that, my lady. Full of vim and vigour — pretty little varmints now they're free of crawlers and dirt.'

He led her to an empty stall at the end of the row. She could hear the excited yapping and increased her pace. All three were standing on their hind legs, tails wagging furiously, waiting to greet her as if she was an old friend.

'I can't believe the difference. I shall go in and become acquainted. I do hope his grace allows us to keep them.' In the excitement of the wedding there had been no opportunity to ask him.

'It's fresh straw, just done, nothing nasty to tread on.'

'That's a relief — but it wouldn't stop me going in.'

'I'll find you a couple of sacks, Lady Sarah. You don't want to mire your gown.'

The puppies were going mad with excitement and with a sack spread on the straw and another on her lap she sat down allowing them to scramble onto her.

All three attempted to lick her face and rolled about in ecstasy as she stroked them. She picked up the bitch that she'd brought back. 'Look at you now. Your coat is the colour of chestnuts and as soft as silk. What a pretty little thing you are.'

She put this one aside and picked up one of the males. 'Well, young man, you're the biggest but certainly not the handsomest.' He was almost twice the weight of the female, had one cocked ear and one flat, his coat was rougher to the touch and a mix of chestnut and black.

The third puppy, also a male, was sitting politely waiting for his turn to be examined. She snapped her fingers and he threw himself into her embrace. He didn't attempt to lick her face but buried his head in her shoulder as if he belonged there.

He too had long silky fur but it was a non-descript mouse brown. In that moment she decided this one would be hers. Whatever Richard thought about the matter she was determined to have him inside with her once he was house-trained.

She leaned against the side of the stall cradling the sleeping animal. The other two curled up in her lap and were soon slumbering as well. Jonah, the head groom, was leaning on the edge of the door watching with interest.

'I reckon they'll not be going anywhere. You need to think of names for them, my lady.'

'This little boy is mine and I'm going to call him Mouse. Lady Beth shall have the female and can think of a name for her — and I'm hoping that the new duchess will lay claim to the third.'

'He ain't going to be no mouse, my lady, I reckon he'll be bigger than the other one if the size of his paws is anything to go by.'

She ran her hand over his soft fur and he stirred and whimpered slightly. 'I don't care how big they get. We've plenty of room and when the new house is built, we'll have even more.' Without waking any of them she slipped them gently onto the sacks and stood up. 'I'll bring Lady Beth down later. Thank you for taking such good care of them.'

Her gown had pieces of straw sticking to the hem but this was soon removed with a brisk shake. The time was still too early for there to be breakfast available so she headed for the library and began to make notes of her plans for the garden party and dance to show to Paul when he next visited.

As expected, her sister was overjoyed to be given a puppy to take care of herself. Sarah thought that Dr Peterson would approve of her decision. It wasn't quite the same as becoming a devoted aunt but would do very well in the meantime.

Tomorrow morning she was determined to ride to the Dower House and discover why neither Mr O'Riley nor Paul had been to collect the post. That afternoon the factor arrived in search of them. When Sarah heard he was enquiring she went to speak to him.

'My lady, I had an appointment to see Mr Marchand this morning and was told neither he nor Mr O'Riley had been seen since yesterday. Do you have any notion where they might be?'

'I do not, I expected them here myself this morning. No doubt he will contact you on his return.'

Mama looked up from her periodical when she entered the drawing room. 'Is something amiss, my dear?'

'I'm not sure. Mr Marchand and Mr O'Riley didn't return to the Dower House last night. Do you think we should send word to Richard?'

Beth was sitting by the window with Miss Westley and her squeal attracted their attention. 'Come and look. Amanda's coming home again. I don't see Richard sitting with her.'

This information was sufficient to get their mother on her feet and the two of them hurried to the window to see for themselves.

'You're right, Beth, she's on her own and returning five days earlier than expected. Something catastrophic must have occurred for Richard to be absent so soon after their marriage.'

Mama was right — Sarah was certain it had something to do with the missing gentlemen.

14

Richard's initial fury at being disturbed on his wedding trip had long since dissipated and was now replaced by the exhilaration he always felt when in action. Rescuing Patrick was a mere bagatelle compared to some of the things he'd done in the past.

He indicated to Paul that he turn up the collar of his coat. It was unfortunate they hadn't been wearing mufflers as these would have been ideal to cover their faces. A flash of white flesh at night was often the death of an unwary soldier.

He crouched and, keeping his head lowered, crept forward alert to the slightest sound. His companion was equally proficient at night manoeuvres and if he didn't know he was behind him would have thought himself alone in the darkness.

Shooting a serving soldier would be a hanging offence even for a duke. The weapon should be enough to deter all but the most foolhardy. There was a slight noise ahead. He froze. There it was again.

He identified the sound as a boot scraping against the cobbles. No groom would be around at this time of night so it had to be a guard.

If he'd heard the noise then he was certain Paul would have done so too. He gestured that they split up. One of them would approach from the front and the other from the rear. His companion moved past him silently and Richard waited for a few minutes to allow him to get into position.

They must overwhelm the guard without him raising the alarm. He reversed his pistol so he was holding it by the barrel and could use the butt as a weapon to knock the man senseless.

They hadn't discussed exactly how this rescue was to be accomplished. Then he heard footsteps approaching from the other side of the yard. For a moment he was horrified then recognised the muttering was coming from Paul.

He was masquerading as a groom come outside to relieve himself.

'What the buggeration do you want? Shove off. There's a privy round the back — use that.' This was the soldier speaking.

Richard was now inside the yard pressed hard against the wall where he couldn't be seen, awaiting his opportunity.

'I ain't going nowhere. This wall will do me just fine.'

There was the unmistakable sound of someone fumbling to unfasten their breeches. His mouth curved. This was a perfect diversion.

The soldier was now on his feet and moving towards Paul with the intention of physically removing him. This was his chance. In three steps he closed the distance and cracked the unsuspecting man on the back of the head. He collapsed without a sound.

'Patrick, we're here to fetch you. Which door are you behind?' Richard waited but there was no response. 'We'll have to unbolt every door and do it quickly. We don't know when they change the guard.' He quickly opened the door in front of them but this was full of a miscellany of what looked like gardening implements. 'I'll go left, you go right. He has to be close to where that man was standing.'

His friend was obviously injured, or gagged and trussed up like a chicken, if he couldn't let them know where he was.

He pulled open the second door and at the far end of the narrow space a shape was slumped. 'Patrick, Patrick, can you move?'

There wasn't even a groan and a flicker of unease ran through him. They would hardly be guarding a corpse so he must be alive, but unless he'd been given a sleeping draught, he was severely concussed.

He dropped to his knees beside him, removed the stiletto he carried in a small sheath inside the top of his Hessian, and slashed the bonds that bound his friend. Patrick's breathing was shallow but steady — thank God.

'He's damned heavy. A dead weight — it's going to be difficult getting him out of here and all but impossible getting him onto a horse.'

Paul had removed the gag from Patrick's mouth. He turned the air blue. 'He has a serious head wound. My fingers are sticky with gore.'

They each put an arm of the unconscious man over their shoulders and heaved. By the time they'd negotiated the narrow doorway they were breathing heavily.

'There's a wheelbarrow, major, in the corner. Not dignified, but it'll do.'

After dumping the patient into the barrow, they dragged the unconscious soldier into the shed that had been Patrick's prison and tied and gagged him with the same ropes that had been used before.

Pushing Patrick was a damn sight easier than carrying him. They'd never have made it to the horses without this rickety vehicle.

'We'll have to tie him across his horse

until we can get him away from here. If they discover he's missing the others will easily overtake us as we'll have to travel slowly.'

'I'll turn their mounts loose, sir, with luck the horses will follow us and that will slow them down sufficiently to allow us to escape.'

Every extra minute it took to secure Patrick and release the horses they were in grave danger of being apprehended. However, he was calm — well used to dealing with danger. He was impressed that Paul was equally composed.

As soon as they were a few miles away he drew rein and swivelled in the saddle to check that Patrick was alive. Having his head hanging one side of a horse and his legs the other was hardly conducive to good health.

'If we take him to Radley he'll be discovered as that's the first place they'll look. I hope the bastard who hit him so hard was the one that I knocked out. I noticed a broken gate back there. I think we should construct some sort of carrier which we can attach to one of our mounts as they're used to pulling a carriage and won't object.'

They carefully lowered Patrick to the ground before removing the gate from its hinges. It was made from poles cut from nearby trees and was light enough for his purpose. The farmer had attempted to keep it together with rope and string which, when unravelled, was ideal for their purpose.

It took them half an hour but he was satisfied his friend would be safer and more comfortable lying prone and being towed along rather than hanging head first from a horse.

They tied him securely to the travois using their three stocks and the remainder of the rope. He thought he was the more proficient horseman so would be the one to ride bareback. They'd used the saddle of his horse to tie the ropes to.

Paul volunteered to lead the animal behind which Patrick was lying. They travelled slowly but their makeshift transport was working as he'd hoped.

After some thought and discussion with his companion he decided Patrick would come home with him after all. They would put him in the servants' quarters and swear the staff to silence.

Just before dawn they turned into the tradesmen's lane that led to Radley. He cantered ahead and roused the butler. By the time Paul appeared there was a trestle, with half a dozen sturdy men to carry it, waiting for Patrick.

★   ★   ★

'I'm capable of temporarily dealing with his head wound,' the major said. 'I've sent someone to fetch Peterson from Ipswich. We can rely on his discretion.'

By the time Patrick was transferred to a bed that was barely long enough for him Paul was seriously concerned about his friend's lack of response. He remained in the room, from which an unfortunate senior footman had been evicted, and assisted the major with removing clothes and bathing the wound.

'That's going to need several sutures, sir, I don't suppose you're proficient with those as well?'

'I've done it from necessity but I don't think Patrick would thank me for doing it now. The pad I've applied to the wound is securely tied to his head and should prevent further bleeding.'

'I'll try and spoon some of this watered wine into his mouth.' Paul managed to get some down him and stepped away satisfied they'd done as much as they could.

The major had decided the fewer people who knew that Patrick was in the attic, being tended to by a reliable man, the better.

'I'm for my bed, Paul. Stay here — there's no need to ride back to the Dower House.'

* * *

Several hours later Paul was woken by the sound of water being poured into a basin in the dressing room. He sat up, yawned, stretched and threw back the covers. He'd slept unclothed and had nothing clean to put on as all his belongings were elsewhere. He didn't relish putting on the soiled garments of yesterday.

'Good morning, sir, I have everything ready for you. His grace provided the necessities. Do you wish me to shave you or will you do it yourself?' The speaker was a young man of about his own age and he thought he might be the footman who had lost his bed to Patrick.

Neither of them was at all embarrassed by his lack of clothes. 'What I'd really like is a bath if one could be arranged.'

'It's ready for you next door, sir.'

He removed the worst of the grime from his person using a washcloth and jug of hot water. Relaxing, even in a hip bath, was exactly what he needed. He emerged a new man and after removing the bristles from his cheeks he was ready to dress.

The footman, he discovered, was called Thomas. 'How is the patient?'

'The doctor has stitched up his head and said he should make a full recovery in time.'

'In time? How long is he anticipating this will take?'

'Two weeks in bed and then a further two weeks recuperating.'

'In which case, Thomas, would you care to take up the position as my valet? At least you will have your own accommodation if you do so.'

The delighted smile that greeted this remark told him he had made the right decision. Paul looked at the overmantel clock. 'Good grief! I should have been at my desk and working hours ago. His grace won't be impressed by my lack of diligence.'

'I don't reckon his grace will be bothered either way, sir. Her grace arrived yesterday.'

There was no need to say any more and they exchanged a smile.

Downstairs the first person he saw was Sarah. 'Mr Marchand, you are living a most unusual life at the moment. Are those Richard's garments you have on?'

'They are, my lady. I expect you know the reason why.' She nodded. 'I don't suppose there's any chance of getting something to eat before I depart?'

'Cook has just been waiting for you to appear. Luncheon is to be served in the breakfast parlour if you care to go there now.'

'This is the most efficient household. Thank you, I'm sharp-set as I haven't eaten since yesterday morning.' He grinned, finding her company a pleasant distraction. 'If you don't count half a meat sandwich last night.'

He thought they would part company but to his surprise she followed him. 'Do you like dogs?'

This was a strange question indeed. 'I do, we always had half a dozen at home.'

'Amanda and I found three half-starved puppies a few days ago and already they're almost recovered and full of energy and spirit. You will see them when you collect your horse later.'

'I'll make a point of looking for them.'

His tone was somewhat sharper than he'd intended but he wished to make it clear he was an employee of her brother and couldn't be a friend of hers. He wouldn't have been so relaxed if he'd known she was going to join him in the breakfast parlour. She remained firmly at his side.

'I have already written down some ideas for the grand event that's to happen next month. Do you wish to see them now or shall I bring them to you in your office later today?'

He was about to explain to her that it would be highly unsuitable for her to visit him anywhere when a footman ran towards them. For a servant to do so must mean it was an emergency of some sort.

'There's four soldiers heading this way, Mr Marchand, and his grace is . . . is not available.'

'Thank you, I'll deal with the matter. How long before they arrive?'

'They're taking their time, sir, I don't reckon they'll be here for another twenty minutes at least.'

270

'Excuse me, my lady, I must speak to your butler.'

'I think, Mr Marchand, that we should take luncheon together as planned and be suitably annoyed when we're disturbed by the intrusion.'

He didn't argue as what she said made perfect sense. If they were to carry this off then they must behave as normal.

'Then lead the way, my dear. I'm hoping that Lady Beth has not been apprised of the new circumstances.'

'She's aware that Amanda came home but not that Richard is now with her. Mama is party to the information and Doctor Peterson's visit was, of course, to see her as she was unwell. That's also the reason for the bridal couple's premature return.'

'I can see that everything was taken care of whilst I was in the land of nod. We can discuss your ideas whilst we eat.'

There was a cold collation set out for them that included a tureen of vegetable soup, freshly baked bread, a basket of hothouse fruits as well as strawberries and an appetising array of condiments to accompany them.

His stomach gurgled loudly, but instead of being shocked by such poor manners his companion laughed.

One might have thought that their appetites would have deserted them in the circumstances but, if anything, the opposite was true. They served themselves but an attentive footman was there if needed.

He was on his second plateful when Foster appeared in the doorway.

'Forgive me for intruding, sir, my lady, but there's a sergeant demanding entry.'

There was the sound of loud voices and then heavy footsteps approached rapidly down the passageway. A barrel-chested, belligerent individual charged in.

'There's an escaped traitor hidden here and I've come to collect him.'

With a sigh Paul put down his cutlery and napkin on the table and stood up. 'Your name?'

'I'm Sergeant Johnson, sent from Horse Guards.'

'I see.' Paul imbued his words with the utmost contempt — every inch an aristocrat and this man's superior. 'There will be a letter complaining of your uncouth behaviour sent by express to London. You will remove yourself from this house and wait outside until Lady Sarah and I have finished our luncheon. I shall then decide whether or not to give you permission to come in and look for this person.'

He was a head taller than the intruder, ten years his junior and although of a slighter build, was fitter and stronger if it came to fisticuffs.

He looked up and saw there were four footmen standing behind Foster — more than enough to evict this individual if necessary.

★　★　★

Sarah was impressed by the way Paul took charge of the situation as if born to it. He really was an attractive gentleman and the more she saw of him the better she liked him. She stood up and moved to stand beside him knowing that this would add to his authority.

'The Duke and Duchess of Denchester will not be impressed if they are disturbed. Mr Marchand is acting in the duke's stead and you would do well to listen to him.'

The truculent sergeant muttered something extremely rude under his breath but retreated, closely followed by Foster and the footmen.

'Shall we continue with our repast? I need to speak to the major and this will be the second time I've disturbed him and I'm not eager to do it.'

'I'm certainly not going to knock on the door. The angrier he is the better as he's quite terrifying when enraged.'

They had just resumed their places when the butler reappeared. 'Forgive me for interrupting you a second time, my lady, sir, but I need to tell you I don't think it will be long before those soldiers attempt to get in by force.'

All desire to eat deserted her. Paul

touched her hand to reassure her. He'd known at once that she was worried.

'Check that all the doors and windows on the ground floor are locked, Foster. That will delay them as I doubt that they have the temerity to break any down.'

'I've already put that in motion, sir. They have weapons and a warrant. I fear we'll have to let them in eventually.'

'We will, but not until his grace is here to take charge. Don't look so terrified, man, I'll go and fetch him myself.'

'Would you like me to come with you? He might be less irascible if I'm there.'

'No, remain down here.' The unmistakable sound of her mama approaching at speed gave him pause. 'Excuse me, my dear, but I'm going to leave you to deal with her grace. One furious aristocrat is more than enough for me.'

His smile made her heart skip a beat and then he was gone through the servants' door thus avoiding any possible contact with her mother.

'Sarah, what's being done about the imminent invasion?'

'Mr Marchand has gone to fetch Richard. He did splendidly and ordered them to leave. We cannot keep them out indefinitely but it has given time for the doors to be locked. Do you think that they will insist on looking absolutely everywhere?'

'I'm certain that they will. I intend to ignore them and pretend that nothing untoward is taking place. Doctor Peterson is a man of good sense and I'm satisfied that Richard has appointed a suitable person to take care of me when necessary.'

'I'm so glad that you like him. Did he make any suggestions as to how to best manage your mood swings?'

'I'm to keep a journal and write down anything of note. My abigail is to do the same. This way he hopes that I'll come to recognise when my mania is about to strike and can make sure that I'm safe in my own apartment and can do no harm to myself or others whilst it lasts.'

To hear her mama talk so openly about her illness was something Sarah had never expected. 'Is the doctor still here? Those horrible soldiers will no doubt wish to question him.'

'He went upstairs to talk to Beth — although I think that he is more interested in Miss Westley than your sister's well-being. I hope I'm mistaken as it would be most inconvenient to lose her now that she is so well settled in the household.'

This was a typical response as her parent was infamous for her lack of sensibility. 'I'm sure that we don't have to worry about this at the moment, Mama, they scarcely know each other and have only met three times.'

As she spoke she could not help but compare Miss Westley's circumstances to her own. Her acquaintance with Paul was equally short, but she was in a fair way to thinking of him as more than an acquaintance.

Her reverie was interrupted by a sharp rap of a fan on her knuckles. 'You are wool-gathering, my girl, and I will not have it. We need to have our wits about us at this difficult time. To think we are about to be overrun by rough soldiers — this would never have happened in your papa's time.'

Sarah was about to agree in the hope of placating her parent but for the second time she was taken aback by what followed.

'I've never had so much excitement in my life. Since Richard became head of the family every day is different and despite my difficulties, I am content with my life nowadays.'

'As am I. Amanda is married to him and I've never seen her so happy. Even Beth seems more settled.'

Their conversation was rudely interrupted by one of the soldiers appearing outside and scowling through the window at them. Initially she recoiled but then recovered her composure and ignored him.

'Mama, might I pour you some coffee? I think I shall have a pastry or two with mine.' Pretending to be unconcerned was the best policy.

'Thank you, my dear, that would be

quite delightful.'

They took their seats at the table and sipped the drink and continued to talk of inconsequential matters. All would have been well if the wretched soldier hadn't decided to bang on the window with the butt of his rifle.

15

Paul didn't hesitate when he reached the major's apartment. He knocked briskly and followed this immediately with an explanation for his intrusion. 'Your grace, the soldiers are here and demanding entry. They have a warrant to search. I cannot delay them for much longer.'

The door opened. 'I'm ready. Let's get on with it. I've sent a letter expressing my disapproval at Patrick's treatment by express. This will reveal the fact that he's with us, but those outside the door won't be aware of it.'

They were halfway down the stairs when he heard the sound of breaking glass, rapidly followed by the screams of the ladies. They completed the distance to the breakfast parlour at a run and shoulder to shoulder burst into the chamber.

The window had been shattered and the bastard who'd done it was already climbing over the windowsill. Paul grabbed him by his throat and threw him backwards. The redcoat landed with a satisfactory thud on the terrace outside. He was about to leap out after him and finish the job when the major grabbed his arm.

'No, Paul, that's enough. So far it's them that have behaved appallingly — let's keep it that way.'

The footman who had been in the room to help serve the ladies was already on his knees to gather up the shards of glass.

'No, don't pick it up in your bare hands you'll be cut,' Sarah told him.

Foster, who must have heard the noise, came in accompanied by another servant holding a dustpan and brush.

Her grace spoke for the first time. 'Come, Sarah my dear, we shall retreat to my apartment and leave this unpleasant business to the gentlemen.'

'Richard, will they insist on searching in the nursery?'

'I expect so, sweetheart, but if you

bring your sister down to her grace's sitting room then she will be safe and comfortable with you all there to keep her calm.'

Paul watched her depart relieved that she hadn't been harmed by the broken window. He was still too shocked by his own reaction to think coherently.

'We have to get this done before there's another incident like this and someone is seriously hurt. Where's Peterson, Sarah?'

'He was in the nursery, Richard, talking to Beth and Miss Westley but no doubt he'll be joining us directly.'

'I'm tempted to open the gun room but think it might exacerbate the situation. Let's get this farce over with.'

The duke seemed sanguine about the outcome — Paul wished he was as optimistic.

'Foster, open the side door. I'll not have these ruffians coming through the front.'

'Yes, your grace. Do you wish me to accompany them?'

'Of course. Have four men with you.

Send one back to fetch me if — well you know what I mean.'

'Shall we join the ladies upstairs or are we to remain here?' Paul wanted to ensure Sarah was kept safe.

'Upstairs. I don't want Beth upset by this search.'

The door to her grace's private sitting room stood open and Paul could hear a lively conversation taking place. There was one male voice so the doctor was with them.

He exchanged a nod with the major, straightened his shoulders, and strolled in as if nothing untoward was taking place.

Amanda had joined the others. Beth was sitting on the window seat with Miss Westley and they were pointing out various landmarks and then the girl was attempting to spell the words.

'I've let them in, they will be here shortly,' the major said as he perched on the side of the chair in which his wife was sitting.

'Mr Marchand, why don't you sit

beside me? I was just regaling the others with your heroics.'

'Lady Sarah, throwing a bully out of the window was hardly heroic.' Paul nodded to the doctor and then half-bowed to the two duchesses. Miss Westley looked across and smiled but Beth ignored him as she was engrossed in her word game.

'Sit down, young man, I wish to have your opinion on the extraordinary ideas my daughter has for this garden party and dance,' the dowager duchess said with a remarkably friendly smile.

Peterson was sitting on an upright chair close to the window which left only the space next to Sarah for him to take. His mouth curved involuntarily. It seemed she was now to be Sarah in his head even if he should continue to use her title when speaking to her.

'Richard, do I need your permission to instigate my ideas or do I have a free hand to arrange things with Mr March- and as I please?'

'Before I answer that question, I need to hear what you propose.'

'There will be two marquees on the lawn in case of inclement weather — one for us and our friends and the other for the villagers and staff. There will be musicians in both places in the evening. I would like to have fireworks as well if that's possible.'

'Go on, I've heard nothing alarming so far.'

Emboldened by the encouragement from the major she then reeled off a series of items that left him wide-eyed and laughing.

'A fire-eater? Stilt-walkers? A fortune teller? Have you run mad?'

Before Sarah could respond to the major's comment her mother interrupted. 'I think it sounds quite delightful. I don't remember ever having such things before.'

Beth rushed over and dropped to her knees in front of the major and stared at him imploringly. 'Please, Richard, do say we can have them. And could we also have a tug-of-war and perhaps a cricket match? I remember seeing both of those at a village fête before.'

'And why not have a horse race and whilst we're about it, sideshows and booths . . . '

Beth took the major's remark as a genuine suggestion and flung her arms around his knees. 'Yes please. Thank you so much, Richard.'

He raised his hands in surrender knowing he had been outmanoeuvred, even if unintentionally. They were all laughing when the arrival of the belligerent sergeant and one of his men interrupted them.

Paul was immediately on his feet as were the major and the doctor. They moved as one to stand in front of the ladies.

Faced by three large, impressive gentlemen the man hesitated. If the others looked as angry as he did then it would be a braver man than this who dared to enter. There was no need for the major to do more than fix them with an arctic stare.

The sergeant muttered something that

could have been an apology and rapidly retreated. Even he would know that Patrick wouldn't be in this apartment.

★ ★ ★

The two soldiers stomped off to continue their search with the butler and a footman close behind. There was a collective sigh of relief when they were out of sight.

'Who were those horrid men, Richard? I didn't like them at all.'

He leaned down and picked Beth from the floor and embraced her. 'They are looking for someone who isn't here. They have been misinformed about this person's whereabouts. They won't bother us again, little one.'

Amanda made room in the chair for her sister to squeeze in meaning that her husband must now find himself somewhere else to sit. 'Don't look so curmudgeonly, my love. I'm sure you'd much rather be following the soldiers about the place, wouldn't you? You can make sure they don't do any damage or intimidate our staff.'

'I'd certainly rather do that than sit here discussing the garden party.' He nodded towards Paul. 'Remain here, in case the other two decide to come this way.'

'Very well, sir, if you're quite sure you don't require me to accompany you.'

'I shall come, Richard, I think them less likely to do something reprehensible with a lady present.'

Peterson resumed his place next to Miss Westley, the dowager excused herself and retreated into her bedchamber leaving him to entertain Sarah.

'Lady Sarah, where do you intend to find these stilt-walkers and so on?'

'There is a Romany camp set up in the grounds of Denchester — they come every summer. I intend to go there and make the arrangements with the tribe leader. The family has always been on good terms with this particular group and I'm certain that they will be only too happy to provide the entertainment

I require.'

'I hope you don't intend to visit the camp without the duke as escort. That would be most unsuitable and possibly dangerous.'

Her sunny smile vanished. 'Whether I go on my own or not is no concern of yours, sir. You forget yourself.'

'No, my lady, I am merely doing the bidding of my employer. You might recall that he asked me to stand in his stead.'

She jumped to her feet. 'That's the outside of enough. I am a woman grown and quite capable of making my own decisions without the interference of . . . of an estate manager.' She said this as if it was an insult and he couldn't prevent the snort of laughter which merely exacerbated the situation.

'How dare you laugh at me. If there's one thing I cannot abide it is being made fun of. I wish that Richard hadn't taken you on as I can see that we are going to be constantly at daggers drawn.'

He stood up and bowed formally. 'Lady Sarah, I apologise if I have offended you.

I shall wait outside in the passageway until your brother returns.'

'Fiddlesticks to that! You'll do no such thing. Sit down and help me decide how many trestles we shall need and how much small beer to brew.'

She was as volatile as a windmill in a storm. He'd thought her a calm, well-mannered young lady but today she was proving him wrong in his assessment of her character. He was tempted to ignore her command but he was rather enjoying this lively exchange and wished to continue it. He spent a pleasant hour exchanging banalities and the more time he spent in her company the better he liked her.

Only then did he remember that they weren't alone in the sitting room and that everything that had been said and done had been heard by Miss Westley and the doctor. He looked across ready to raise an eyebrow or shrug but they were so engrossed in some sort of game with Beth that they had obviously not been aware of what had just transpired.

His glance across the room was noticed by Sarah. Her look of horror was quite comical. A becoming flush spread from her neck to her cheeks and he found it quite endearing.

'It's all right, my lady, our conversation wasn't overheard.'

'I apologise for being so sharp with you earlier. I'm on edge and won't be able to relax until those wretched men have gone and our guest is safe.' She leaned forward confidingly. 'I cannot understand why they would have hurt him so badly. After all, isn't the purpose of his arrest that he can be re-enlisted and sent to serve that general?'

'Exactly so. However, I think Mr O'Riley wouldn't come willingly so the only way they could transport him was to render him unconscious.'

'Isn't his enlistment over now? I know that a deserter can be arrested even years after his defection but surely the intervention of the Duke of Denchester should count for something?'

The major spoke from behind them

making them both jump. 'I should think that it does, my dear. The soldiers have left satisfied that we're not harbouring the man they seek.'

Amanda drifted in and took Beth's hand. 'It's time for the grown-ups to dress for dinner, my love. You must go upstairs for tea.'

'Will you come and kiss me good night, Amanda? Mama doesn't do it anymore.'

'I will. Now run along with Miss Westley like a good girl.'

The doctor bowed. 'I too must depart. I'm relieved they didn't wish to interview me.'

'Please, Doctor Peterson, why don't you stay for dinner?'

'That's kind, your grace, but I must return as I might well have visits to make before it's too dark to go out.'

Paul thought that if Miss Westley had been included in the dinner invitation the man would have agreed with alacrity.

'Doctor Peterson, if you would be kind enough to wait for a few minutes before you leave, I wish to check that my mother is well. It's unlike her to rest for so long on an afternoon.'

Paul had been wondering this himself and was relieved that the physician was on hand. Amanda returned with a smile. 'She's dressing for dinner. It would seem that she had no wish to be part of another confrontation.'

'I too must go. I have already out-stayed my welcome.'

'I insist that you stay, Paul. Then I'll not have to change. Damn silly, if you ask me, changing one's clothes so often.' The major smiled making him look more approachable. Marriage was obviously good for him.

★ ★ ★

Sarah took more care with her appear-ance that evening. They didn't put on evening wear as Richard refused to wear his — if he had his way, they would all remain in whatever they put on when they got up. He had compromised on this point with Mama. She had agreed to dine later if he would at least change from his riding clothes into something a little smarter.

'There, my lady, I'm done. The turquoise necklace and ear bobs complement your gown perfectly.'

'I shan't require your attention further tonight. I can remove this gown without assistance. You may have the evening free. Put out my habit for the morning.'

As always, she ran lightly upstairs in order to kiss Beth good night. 'You look very pretty, Sarah, I think that's my favourite colour on you. I don't remember what it's called.'

'*Eau de Nil*, darling, but is also known as duck-egg blue which is far easier to recall. I'm going to ride over to Denchester tomorrow morning. Do you wish to accompany me on your pony? It's so long since you've ridden.'

'I would, I would. Can Miss Westley come too?'

'I don't ride, Lady Beth, it's a skill I never had the opportunity to learn.'

'Can you teach her, Sarah? Then she

can come out with me every morning.'

'I'm not skilled enough to teach anyone but I'm sure there's someone here who can do that if you would like to learn, Miss Westley?'

'I'd like nothing better. Thank you, I do appreciate being treated as one of the family.'

Sarah picked up her skirt and made her way to the drawing room where she could hear male voices — but not that of her mother or sister. She was reluctant to go in without their support. She loved Richard but he could be rather alarming and she certainly didn't wish to spend time with Paul. He was equally unsettling but in quite a different way.

Richard called from the drawing room. 'Don't dither about out there, Sarah, come in and join us.'

How had he known she was there as he couldn't see her?

She scowled at him on her entrance. 'Do you have mystical powers? I don't understand how you knew I was there.'

He laughed and pointed to the

window. 'Your reflection was quite clear in that. I won't offer you champagne, but there's that revolting orgeat or lemonade.'

'Lemonade, thank you. I agree with you about the orgeat. But if forced to choose I would drink that rather than sherry wine which is even more unpalatable.'

Amanda and Mama came in and the conversation turned to the invasion by the soldiers and its happy outcome. 'Is Mr O'Riley conscious yet?'

'He came around just before I came down, Sarah. His wits were clear and I'm sure he'll have made a full recovery far quicker than Peterson suggested,' Richard told her.

Conversation over dinner was lively and enjoyable and when Amanda stood up the two gentlemen did also. Mama frowned — she was a stickler for protocol and thought that they should remain behind and drink port even if they didn't wish to.

'Richard, Miss Westley expressed a

desire to learn to ride. Beth was eager for her to accompany her. Do you give your permission?'

'I'd instruct her myself if I had the time. Paul, could you do it for me?'

'I'd be delighted to, sir. However, it will have to be after I've completed the necessary duties involved with my position.'

Her grace turned to Amanda. 'You could do it, my dear, far more suitable. Would you play for us? I find music so relaxing. Doctor Peterson thinks that I'm less likely to have unpleasant episodes if I remain calm.'

'I'd be delighted to.' Richard got to his feet. 'No, my love, I'll play without music so there's no need for you to stand beside me.'

The magnificent piano, brought over from Denchester, had been wheeled to the far end of the drawing room. Her sister settled on the piano seat and soon the room was filled with the liquid notes of a piece she didn't recognise.

Sarah had fully intended to ask Richard's permission to visit the Romany camp but it quite slipped her mind. Only later, as she was drifting off to sleep did she recall the words of warning given to her by Paul — that on no account should she go there unaccompanied by either himself or Richard.

He had already stated quite unequivocally that he was too busy with his duties to teach Miss Westley as was Richard, so even if they wanted to, they couldn't come with her. Two grooms would be more than adequate.

The next morning she collected Beth and together they made their way to the stables. She had already sent word for her docile mare and Beth's pony to be ready.

The sun was shining, there was a light breeze, and she considered it a perfect day for a gentle hack of scarcely two miles in either direction.

'We're going to Denchester to see how the building of the new house is progressing.'

One of the grooms who was accompanying them, nodded. 'I can take you through the woods and fields, my lady, and avoid the main thoroughfare if you would prefer that.'

'I would. I've no wish for us to encounter a mail coach on Lady Beth's first outing since last year.'

She was pleased to see that there was an extra rein attached to the bit of Beth's mount. It was wise to be prepared for any eventuality. If her sister became agitated then one of the grooms could safely lead her horse.

16

Paul was at his desk in the Dower House at first light. He had shirked his responsibilities yesterday and intended to make up for it today. He was so engrossed that the time flew and he didn't stir from his position until he was disturbed by the duke striding in.

'I'd like your opinion on a change to the master plan that the architects have suggested. Come with me, you need to take a break as you've been working since dawn without respite.'

How the hell his employer was aware of that fact, Paul had no idea. 'I'll be delighted to come with you, major. I was about to stop as I've completed everything that needed to be done.'

'There's no need to ride — it's a short walk.'

The noise from the building site didn't disturb him unduly, but then he was working behind closed windows half a mile away. He was impressed that the labourers were progressing so fast and already the shape of the building was recognisable.

'Are the architects here permanently, major, or do they just come if needed?'

'They visit periodically and when I require to see them. They've suggested that I include an orangery to the south wall where we can grow exotic fruit and have flowers for the house all year round.'

The major's lack of enthusiasm made Paul smile. 'It sounds an excellent notion — one that her grace will approve of.'

'Do you think so? I don't know if there was one originally as I didn't spend more than an hour or two inside before it was demolished. I know there's one at our present home. I thought to do without that sort of nonsense. But I'll be guided by you. If you think Amanda would expect to find such a place in her new home then I'll give them permission to continue.'

'Forgive me for saying so, sir, but

wouldn't you do better to consult her grace rather than myself?'

'My wife told me to do whatever I wanted as she was confident that I'd make the right decision. She's not like other women — she doesn't want to be the height of fashion here. She just wants a comfortable family home for all of us.'

A flash of dapple grey caught Paul's attention at the far side of the park. His vision was excellent and he shaded his eyes in order to see more clearly. A feeling of dread settled in his stomach.

'Major, isn't that that Lady Sarah's horse? It's riderless.'

'God dammit to hell — you're right.'

The duke set off at a flat run towards the stables. He yelled that the horses be saddled as soon as he was near enough for his parade ground voice to carry.

The duke's stallion was ready but his was missing a saddle. Paul vaulted on, grabbed the reins and the two of them galloped towards the loose mare.

He didn't need to be told to reduce the pace and to take the path that would take him in front of the loose animal whilst the major approached from the side. If the mare spooked his gelding would block her from bolting.

There was no need for the stealthy approach as the mare, on seeing the stallion, trotted eagerly towards him. Paul waited until the major held the reins before cantering up to join him. There was no blood on the saddle. The constriction around his chest released a little.

'What the devil is Sarah doing so far from home?'

'She mentioned that she was intending to visit the Romany camp but I told her she mustn't do so without your permission. I take it she didn't secure this.'

'She wouldn't be so stupid as to ride out without grooms in attendance, especially as she was bringing Beth with her.'

Paul sniffed and could faintly detect the smell of smoke. 'I'm beginning to think that this is no emergency, but carelessness on the part of the grooms. The mare must have pulled herself free from her tether and wandered off from the camp and her absence hasn't been noted.'

'That's the most likely explanation and the one I wish to believe. I don't know exactly where the camp is situated but, when riding around the park, I noticed a small glade with a stream running through it. That would be the perfect place for their caravans and horses as they have water and grazing.'

He made no mention of Paul's lack of a saddle but then neither did he ask him to lead the spare horse. As they approached the camp dogs started to bark and the smell of roasting meat and herbs drifted towards them through the trees.

Then Sarah suddenly appeared in front of them. She looked neither disconcerted nor apologetic. 'Marco, the leader here, said you were coming and that you'd found Star. We're just about to eat lunch — I believe it to be rabbit.'

He slid to the floor and stepped forward so he could take the reins of the other two animals leaving Sarah's guardian free to explain to her exactly where she'd stepped out of line. He doubted it would be an enjoyable experience for her.

As he led the horses to join the others tethered at the far side of the encampment, he was a little sorry for Sarah, but she deserved to be taken to task for her recklessness. He would find the grooms and deal with them but first he would find Beth and make sure she was happy here.

Two swarthy men nodded, smiled, and held out their hands to take the reins he was holding. He handed them over confident they would be well looked after. There were a dozen or more horses and ponies in a makeshift corral at the far side of the busy camp and every coat was glossy and every animal in good health. Beth's pony and those of the grooms were amongst them.

He scanned the score or more of assorted members of this extended family and immediately saw her golden curls amongst the black-haired children. She was sitting with them and they were playing some sort of game with ribbons and sticks.

Satisfied she didn't require him he turned his attention to the errant servants. Their job was to guard not only the horses but also those that rode them. A wizened old lady, who was stirring an aromatic pot of vegetables over a fire, gave him a toothless grin and nodded towards the far end of the camp from which he could now hear drunken laughter coming.

He strode across the trodden grass and walked between the two colourful caravans the old crone had indicated. The missing men were sprawled against the rear wheels sharing a leather bottle of some home brewed alcohol. He'd expected some of the Romany men to be with them but they were drinking alone. He had a nasty suspicion that they'd found the leather bottle and helped themselves.

Paul was estate manager, had the

authority to hire and fire tenants and farm workers — however, he wasn't sure if this extended to the personal staff the duke.

★ ★ ★

Sarah began to feel a little uneasy as the silence between herself and Richard lengthened. She had been having such an enjoyable time, as had her sister, had been made most welcome by these friendly people and had quite forgotten that her behaviour might be disapproved of.

'Richard, are you very cross with me? Mr Marchand did say I should ask your permission before I came but I forgot to do so. Should I not be here?'

Still he said nothing and suddenly she realised he was so angry he didn't trust himself to speak. Her bladder almost emptied but then sanity returned. He might roar at her, give her an almighty bear-garden jaw, but he would never raise his hand.

'I'm very sorry . . .'

'Sorry? You have no idea how sorry you will be for coming here without permission. Paul told you quite clearly that this trip couldn't happen without my being with you and yet you chose to ignore these words.'

'Mr Marchand has no authority over me.'

'Perfectly true, but I am your guardian, head of your family, and you knew very well you were breaking every rule today.'

She was about to interrupt again but then thought better of it. He continued to stare at her as if she was something unpleasant he had stepped in. She shifted from foot to foot no longer optimistic that she was going to escape with only a severe set down.

'You will remain in your apartment and take your meals on trays. You will not appear downstairs, but remain in your chambers. You will not ride out again. This will continue until I consider that you've learned your lesson.'

She was unable to respond coherently. He was treating her like a child but now wasn't the time to say so.

'Well, young lady, do you understand?'

She nodded and swallowed the lump in her throat.

'Good. Remain here whilst I collect your sister.' He stepped around her and she was about to follow him as she had no wish to stand about on her own in the trees. He spoke without turning. 'I don't agree with physical punishment for those weaker than myself but in your case I'll make an exception if you have the temerity to disobey.'

He vanished into the camp leaving her stunned by his last remark. Her knees gave way and she slithered down the tree trunk until she was in a miserable heap at the bottom.

Why had he been so harsh? How could he threaten to beat her? Scalding tears trickled down her cheeks and she gulped and tried to hold them back. Sometime later a soft cloth was pushed into her hand.

'Here, sweetheart, take this and dry your eyes.'

Paul had found her and was here to offer support and comfort. She was incapable of speech; sobs shook her and she turned towards him. He scooped her up and settled her on his lap and his shirt was sodden by the time she recovered her composure.

'He wouldn't have beaten you; he loves you, but you scared us both. It was his anger and relief that you were unharmed that made him so stern.'

'I don't understand. How did I scare you?'

As soon as he explained the circumstances she understood. She scrambled to her feet, blew her nose noisily on his handkerchief, and then faced him. 'You did tell me I shouldn't do this. Richard was right to be so angry. Is my face very red? I must go and find him and beg for his forgiveness. I cannot bear that I caused you both so much unnecessary distress by my selfishness.'

'You are prepared to risk being put

across his knee in order to do this?'

She stamped her foot. 'You just told me, sir, that it was an idle threat. Which is it?'

'You must decide that, Sarah.'

She was about to protest then saw his lips twitch. 'This is hardly the time for jollity, Mr Marchand. I don't like you, I don't like you at all. You are the most annoying gentleman.'

'I know, for I've often been told that before. Come, Sarah, let me escort you to the gentleman in question. That way I can protect you from his wrath if necessary.'

Instead of answering she kicked him hard in the shin and ran away laughing. Despite the fact that he was wearing boots he would have a bruise. It served him right for teasing her.

He caught up easily, caught her hand and put it on his arm. His smile made her toes curl in her boots. 'Would you like to know what happened to the grooms who were supposed to be taking care of your horses?'

'I would indeed. To have let Star get free is a gross dereliction of their duties.'

'I found them drunk behind one of the caravans. They had purloined a leather bottle of home-made brew.'

'Good heavens! That's dreadful — what did you do?'

'I dismissed them without reference and tipped a bucket of something extremely unpleasant over their heads.'

She looked up at him and returned his smile. 'I do hope they won't be riding back with us.'

'They won't be riding anywhere. They will walk back to collect their belongings and any back wages.'

Richard's voice carried to them from across the clearing and she couldn't stop her hand clenching. Immediately Paul put his own over her fingers.

'He will already have forgiven you. He has a fearsome temper but it doesn't last for long.'

'He said I'm to be confined to my apartment until he gives me leave to come down.'

'Then I'm quite certain that you'll be given permission to resume your normal life tomorrow.'

His quiet reassurance was enough to calm her nerves. For some reason she was reluctant to let go of his arm and he seemed in no hurry to release her. Her sister was happily talking to Richard and he seemed to be drinking something from a silver mug with great enjoyment.

Somehow, he sensed they were looking at him and looked up. His smile was genuine and he beckoned them over.

'I was about to come and look for you both. There's no need to look so apprehensive, sweetheart, I've recovered my temper now. Have you come to apologise again?'

Finally, she released her hold on Paul's arm. She stepped forward and curtsied. 'I most humbly apologise for my stupidity, your grace, and beg your forgiveness.'

He rose smoothly to his feet and held out his arms and she ran into them. He held her close. 'You are a baggage, my dear, and should know better than to do

313

such things. I thought you the sensible member of the family.'

She stepped away. 'I thought so too, Richard, but for some reason these past two weeks I've been behaving out of character. Look, I believe we've been invited to sit down and eat.'

The meal was quite delicious, the juices from the meat were mopped up with bread baked in a clay oven in the centre of the fire. For a duke and his family to be eating so informally and in such a setting would scandalise members of the *ton*, but she cared not for that.

When they departed an hour later arrangements had been finalised for the Romanies to come to the garden party and provide the entertainment.

Beth rode next to Richard and two boys from the camp came with them on their ponies each one leading a spare horse. If one ignored the unpleasant interlude with Richard it had been a most enjoyable outing. Paul returned to the Dower House and she was sorry to see him depart.

As she was about to run upstairs and change her brother touched her arm. 'Remember, Sarah, you remain in your rooms until I tell you otherwise.' His tone was bland but she knew he meant every word and she wasn't going to argue.

★ ★ ★

Richard went in search of his wife eager to regale her with the events of the day. She was waiting for him in their bed-chamber.

'Two grooms returned here covered in human excrement. They insist that Paul did it. What exactly had they done to deserve such treatment?'

She was laughing with him by the time he'd finished his explanation. 'I'm curious, darling girl, as to why you're sitting in your petticoats at this time of the day.'

'I would have thought that was obvious, your grace. I was waiting for your return.'

A considerable time later, freshly bathed and dressed they emerged from

315

the apartment and made their way to the drawing room. As Sarah wouldn't be joining them there would only be the three of them to dine tonight.

'There you are, I've been waiting this age for you to descend. I'm well aware that you've only been married a short while but bedroom sport in the afternoon is not something that I approve of.' His mother-in-law was looking more prune-faced than usual and gave him a frosty nod.

He laughed and so did his wife. He left it to Amanda to smooth things over and went to speak to Foster.

'Lady Sarah will require a tray in her apartment tonight. Therefore, we will dine on the terrace. It's a perfect night for such a venture.'

The butler hurried away to organise this unusual request and Richard wandered back to sit beside his beloved. He waited for a pause in the conversation before speaking.

'I believe that Paul and Sarah are going to make a match of it and far sooner than any of us expected. You only have to look at them together to see that they are besotted with each other.' If he'd expected this announcement to receive shocked exclamations, he would have been disappointed.

'My darling Richard, we were just discussing that very thing. I know they've only been acquainted for three weeks but Mama and I believe their love is genuine. However, I'm not sure that he will consider himself a suitable match for Sarah.'

'If we consider him good enough to become part of this family then he'll have to accept our verdict. I'll invite him to dine with us tomorrow night — in fact, Mama, with your permission I'll include Peterson and Miss Westley.'

'Good heavens, young man, are you determined to play matchmaker? What will we do about Beth if Miss Westley is to marry the doctor? Where will Sarah and Mr Marchand reside? This might be a commodious establishment but it isn't big enough for three families.'

'Mama, we have a dozen bedchambers, numerous reception rooms and acres of park. More than sufficient for eight adults — nine if you count Patrick amongst our number.'

'Amanda, surely you are not suggesting that Miss Westley should remain under this roof if she is married to the doctor? He will wish her to reside in Ipswich with him — a wife's place is with her husband.'

'Your grace, you must not become agitated about this. We're speculating — have no actual evidence that there are to be any further nuptials. Time enough to consider the details when it happens, don't you think?'

'Richard, have you arranged for us to eat outside? How delightful — I can't think of anything better on such a beautiful evening. Sarah will be sad to be excluded.' His beloved deftly turned the conversation to a safer topic.

'I hope you're not suggesting that I allow her to avoid any sort of punishment for her rash behaviour?'

'No, my love, merely stating that my sister will be sorry to have missed it. Come, I believe that dinner is about to be served on the terrace.'

17

Paul was in two minds whether to accept the invitation to dine with the family but decided a refusal might be misconstrued and considered impolite. The note from Amanda said that they were dressing for dinner tonight. If she hadn't warned him, he would have appeared too informally.

The first of his new outfits had arrived and it was fortuitous that one of these was his evening rig. His valet had settled into his role and was eager to turn out his new master looking his best.

'You'll need to drive yourself, sir, you can't ride in evening clothes.'

'There's a gig in the coach house that will be perfect for such an excursion as long as one of the horses here will go under harness.'

'Don't know about that, sir, but I reckon Sid, the groom, will sort something out for you.'

'I'll ask him now. I won't be back

until it's time for me to change. I'll need quantities of hot water as I've no intention of arriving smelling of the stables.' Today he was visiting two nearby farms and the village. He would be in the saddle all day.

★ ★ ★

On his return he saw the gig, sparkling after a thorough clean, was waiting to be attached to a suitable carriage horse. The gelding he'd been riding all day was taken to be groomed, fed and watered before being turned out into the meadow.

'Sid, have we something here to pull this vehicle?'

'I haven't, sir, but I sent the lad to fetch one that will do. He ain't back yet from the stud, but I reckon he'll be here soon.'

'Good. I need to leave in an hour and a half.'

After completing his ablutions, he shaved — this was something he preferred to do for himself. He'd adopted the recent fashion of trousers and evening slippers rather than knee breeches and silk stockings. When Thomas had finished fussing with his stock Paul stood up not bothering to check his appearance in the mirror. Why else did one have a valet if it wasn't to see that one was turned out impeccably?

There was a lively chestnut gelding between the shafts which he viewed with some suspicion. The beast tried to take a lump from his shoulder when he walked past.

'Are you quite sure this horse is safe to drive?'

The groom grinned and nodded vigorously. 'He's a mite excitable, sir, but he'll settle once you've travelled a mile or two.'

Paul climbed into the vehicle, released the brake and snapped the whip above the horse's laid-back ears. He could feel the tension coming through the reins and deliberately relaxed his hands. The horse would sense any nervousness on his part and behave accordingly.

The gelding leaned into the traces and moved away smoothly. Sid was right, once they were in motion his ears flicked forwards, his head came up and he appeared to be enjoying the experience. The short journey was covered without incident and he was sanguine that his fears were unfounded.

He jumped from the gig, tossed his driving cape, gloves and beaver onto the seat and quickly pulled on his white evening gloves. He found wearing gloves indoors a decidedly silly practice but knew it was *de rigueur*. If the major was barehanded then these would be tossed aside immediately.

The front door opened as he approached and the butler himself was there to bow him in. 'His grace has requested that you join him on the terrace, Mr Marchand.'

'Thank you, I'll find my own way.' Paul could hear voices through the open French doors in the drawing room and hurried towards them. He wasn't tardy so the others must be down early.

He paused in the doorway. He smiled in relief as he'd feared that Sarah might still be confined to quarters. She was wearing a lovely confection, a gossamer-thin material of silver shimmered over an underskirt of a blue, the colour of her eyes.

She saw him at once and came towards him her eyes alight with pleasure. 'Mr Marchand, I've not seen you in evening clothes before and I must say you look very handsome in black and white.' She curtsied and he bowed.

'I thank you for your compliment, my lady. Might I be permitted to say that you look lovely tonight. That ensemble is perfect with your colouring.'

She smiled playfully and tapped him on his gloved hand with her fan. 'Are you suggesting, sir, that on other occasions I wasn't looking at all attractive? That only the addition of this gown has changed your opinion of my appearance?'

His laughter at her nonsense turned the attention of the others towards them.

He didn't give a damn what they thought any more — in a blinding moment of clarity he understood that he was neck and crop in love with this wonderful girl. Despite his protestations to the contrary to the major a short while ago he was determined to pursue this wonderful girl and marry her at the earliest opportunity.

'Fishing for compliments, my lady? You're the most beautiful girl I've ever set eyes on. You will outshine anyone else whatever you're wearing.' He'd been about to say in her petticoats but stopped himself in time as this might have been considered wildly inappropriate by anyone listening to their conversation.

'I wish to retract what I said yesterday about not liking you. I find that quite the opposite is true.' Her smile was blinding as she continued. 'I wish you to call me by my given name again and dispense with the formality. I noticed that Richard already calls you Paul. Might I be permitted to do the same?'

'I am forced to admit that I was still

calling you Sarah in my head. This must be the most unconventional ducal family in the country.'

She opened her fan and hid her face behind it before answering. 'Apart from my dear mother of course. She is a stickler for etiquette and it's she you must convince of your suitability.' Instantly she realised what she'd said and her eyes widened and colour fled from her cheeks.

He took her hand and pulled her back through the door so they were more private. 'My love, I thought it too soon to mention my feelings for you. I love you and if I can persuade your formidable guardian to accept my suit, I will make you an offer.'

Richard spoke from behind them. He had an unpleasant habit of creeping up on a fellow when least expected. 'I rather think, my friend, that it's my sister you must persuade not me. I'll not be the one marrying you after all.'

He took his cue and dropped to one knee. 'Sarah, will you do me the honour of becoming my wife? I cannot offer you luxury or . . .'

'Fiddlesticks to that, Paul. Once we're married my fortune will be yours and we'll have more than enough to live in a very comfortable manner.'

This wasn't the accepted response to a proposal but it was good enough for him. He surged to his feet and snatched her up. She came into his arms as if meant to be there and he kissed her tenderly.

'Congratulations, Paul. I thought this romance would take longer to reach fruition but I think the sooner the two of you are married the better.'

Sarah remained within his embrace but turned to look at her brother. 'Are you suggesting that we might do something improper before the knot is tied?'

'No, sweetheart, it's that you've been running me ragged and I'd much prefer to hand your care over to someone else.' His face was stern but his eyes were dancing. 'As your husband Paul will have the right to apply whatever discipline he feels suitable.'

'He'd no sooner chastise me physically

than you would, Richard. Did you know this proposal was likely to come and that's why we were told to change tonight?'

'I thought it likely after what I've seen yesterday. Shall we go in and announce the good news to the others?'

★ ★ ★

Sarah walked in beside her future husband and there was no need for anything to be announced. The champagne was already waiting on a tray and Amanda rushed across and embraced her.

'I'm so happy for you. To think that a short time ago you and Paul had yet to meet.' She turned to him and took his hands. 'Welcome to the family. Are you planning to marry soon or have a long engagement so that you can get to know each other better?'

'This has happened so unexpectedly, your grace . . . '

'I am Amanda to you now. We don't stand on ceremony in this family as no doubt you have noticed.'

'Thank you, Amanda. I was trying to say that we've not had time to discuss anything. We can do that tomorrow.'

Sarah was so happy she thought she might actually float into the air if he hadn't been holding her hand. 'Richard wants us to get married as soon as possible as he finds me a nuisance and wishes to pass me on to Paul.'

This sally was greeted with laughter as she'd intended. She led him over to her parent who wasn't looking particularly overjoyed at the news. 'I hope that you're as happy with my betrothal as I am, Mama.'

'I approve of the engagement, my dear, but not of the indecent haste with which it's been agreed. In my day a young lady would not dream of accepting an offer until she had been acquainted with the gentleman for several months.'

Paul pulled round a chair and sat down next to his future mother-in-law. 'Your grace, I understand your concerns. Sometimes it takes longer for a couple to recognise that they love each other but in our case it happened almost instantly.'

'Good heavens, young man, love has nothing to do with it. A young lady with the pedigree of my daughter, if she were to appear on the marriage mart in London, would have every eligible gentleman at her feet. She could then select a few that were suitable and only allow herself to fall in love with one of those.'

Sarah was about to protest but Paul shook his head slightly indicating that he was handling the situation himself. 'If only it were as simple as that, your grace, then there would be more happy marriages and less discord. Love is like a disease and one cannot know when one might catch it. Sarah and I were struck down so quickly we had no time to consider the consequences.'

'If my daughter is set on this union then I'll not stand in her way. You have my consent but not my blessing.'

'Thank you, your grace.' He bowed and withdrew leaving Sarah to continue the conversation in private.

'Mama, when you get to know him

better you'll see that he's the perfect match for me. I know I told everyone that I had no intention of marrying for another year at least but as Paul said, things changed when he arrived in our lives.'

'I must own that you look radiant, my dear, and your happiness is paramount. Despite my reservations I think that perhaps you have met the gentleman who will make you happy. You will be pleased to know that I do not for one minute consider that he is marrying you for your fortune.'

'Neither do I, Mama. I think seeing how Richard so quickly accepted him into the household and dispensed with formality reinforced my belief that Paul's lack of fortune was no barrier.'

Her mother looked towards the terrace and for the first time that evening her smile was genuine. 'We dined outside last night and it was most enjoyable. I see Richard has arranged for us to do the same tonight. I could become accustomed to *al fresco* dining whilst the weather is clement.'

The conversation was interrupted by the arrival of her younger sister accompanied by a nursemaid. Beth rushed over to her and Sarah held her close.

'Richard said I can come down for a little while and congratulate you on your betrothal to Mr Marchand. Will you live in the Dower House with him when you're married?'

'I don't know, sweetheart, we haven't had time to discuss it yet. Would you like to see outside where there's been a table laid for dinner?'

'I would, I would. Can I stay for dinner?'

Richard overheard this question. 'You can remain for the first course, Beth, but after that you must go up. Remember, you've already had your tea and won't want to sit through three courses with us.'

Beth pouted and glared across the room. 'Why is Miss Westley not talking to me? She shouldn't be spending so much time with Doctor Peterson.'

Fortunately, her voice didn't carry. 'Beth, if you're going to behave badly you can retire immediately.'

Her sister snatched her hand away and stamped her foot. Were they going to get the unedifying spectacle of a tantrum?

Richard stepped in. He put his arm around her waist and before she could protest had whisked her from the room. The nursemaid was obliged to run in order to keep up with them. Miss Westley had been so engrossed in her conversation that she was unaware of what had transpired.

'I'll go up with her, Lady Sarah, forgive me for not paying more attention to my charge.'

Amanda shook her head. 'No, remain here with us. Richard will deal with it.'

In fact he was back in less than one quarter of an hour. 'Beth sends her apologies for her bad behaviour. I told her that if she's good tomorrow, she can join us on the terrace.'

Foster announced that dinner was served and Paul led her out and took his place beside her. She scarcely knew what she ate but she was sure the food was delicious.

When the final dish was removed Paul suggested that they take a stroll around the garden whilst it was still light enough to see.

'There's a summerhouse in the rose garden which will be perfect for us to sit in and discuss our future together.' There was no need to ask anyone's permission — from now on the only gentleman to whom she must refer was him.

They walked hand in hand neither feeling the need for conversation. The evening chorus from the blackbirds filled the air and was a perfect accompaniment to their walk.

'Here we are, we can sit on the stone bench.'

He quickly spread his handkerchief for her so that she wouldn't mire her gown. The heady aroma of honeysuckle and roses surrounded them. With a sigh of pleasure she leaned against him and he put his arm around her waist, drawing her closer.

'Are you quite sure about this, darling? We're barely acquainted — is that sufficient time for you to commit yourself to spending the rest of your life with me?'

'I might ask you the same question. In the normal way of things, a young lady would perhaps spend an hour or two in the company of her future husband and would always be chaperoned. I consider that we've spent more time together than is usual, not less, as you've been living in the same house as me.'

'It might seem that way, but we've actually only spent a few hours together. I know that I'll never change my mind but I want to give you the opportunity to do so before you make a lifelong commitment.'

'How can you say that? You told my mother that we're meant to be together that we're irrevocably in love. Why are you changing your mind?'

'Darling, I've not changed my mind. I'm six years your senior, have far more experience of the world than you, I don't wish to rush you into anything you might regret.'

She could think of only one way to convince him she was more than ready to take this step. She pressed herself against him, linked her hands around his neck and pulled his head down so she could kiss him.

He resisted her scandalous advance for a few seconds then lifted her onto his lap and she was swept away, forgot everything but the joy of his lips on hers. His heat burnt through her thin gown. His hands were caressing her face, her back, whilst his lips travelled from her mouth to the curve of her bosom.

Then he released her abruptly and was on his feet standing with his back to her. His breathing sounded laboured — her own was little better.

'Go in, my love, before I do something that we'll both regret.'

'I don't wish to wait to marry you.'

Slowly he turned to face her, but remained more than an arm's length from her. 'I know that, sweetheart, but

I must do the right thing for both of us.'

She ignored his raised hand and stepped closer to him. 'If you don't agree to marry me this summer I shall come to your bedchamber and force you to do so.'

His eyes darkened but he didn't act on his desire. 'I surrender. If you did that your brother would run me through. Shall we marry and make the garden party our celebration?'

'Mama will have a conniption fit, but yes, that would be absolutely perfect.'

★ ★ ★

The duke and his duchess had, unknown to the couple, been standing close by listening to this exchange. His grace turned to her with relief.

'A second wedding within a month, my love. Your sister is more like you than I realised.'

'I think it behoves you to set more men to finish our new home as this one will be somewhat overcrowded, especially if both Sarah and I are blessed with babies next year.'

'If you and I are not parents it won't be for lack of application on our part.'

They strolled in but once inside they increased their pace and were running by the time they reached their apartment.